"For God so loved the world, that he gave his
only-begotten Son, that whosoever believes in
him should not perish, but have eternal life."
John 3:16

✝ **This book is gladly donated by** ✝
Immanuel Lutheran Church
14103 Saratoga Ave., Saratoga, CA 95070
(408) 867-0822

ONCE THE HODJA

ONCE THE HODJA

By
ALICE GEER KELSEY

Illustrated by

Frank Dobias

DAVID McKAY COMPANY, INC.

New York

ONCE THE HODJA

COPYRIGHT • 1943
BY ALICE GEER KELSEY

First Edition December 1943
Reprinted August 1944
January 1945, September 1949
August 1952, October 1954
March 1956, April 1958, 1960
July 1962
August 1964
February 1967
October 1968

Printed in the United States of America

To

PAUL, EDITH, OLIVE, AND MARTHA

FOREWORD

FIVE centuries ago, so runs the tale, a Turkish schoolmaster was berating a group of his pupils for a prank. One by one he called them to him to ask what part each had had in the mischief. Solemnly he pronounced a punishment to fit each crime.

At last came the turn of a particularly lively pupil, Nasr-ed-Din.

"And what did you do?" demanded the schoolmaster.

"Nothing." Nasr-ed-Din shrugged. "All I did was to watch and laugh."

The schoolmaster pondered a moment and hit upon the perfect punishment for one who merely watched and laughed.

"As long as the world lasts, people will laugh at you!"

For five centuries the people of Turkey, and of all the Near East, have been laughing at Nasr-ed-Din — and still they laugh. The humorous folklore of the nation has been hung upon the name of Nasr-ed-Din, who, on becoming a teacher-priest, added the honorary title of Hodja to his name. Young and old, rich and poor, ignorant and learned, break into a grin of anticipation whenever they hear, "That reminds me of a Nasr-ed-Din Hodja story!" There are hundreds of these stories. In many of them the Hodja's patient, long-eared donkey has a part, for the Hodja, like the Turkish villager of today, has one friend upon whom he can depend — his donkey.

Some of these stories are thought to be real happenings. Nobody knows, and nobody cares, which are history and which are legend. It is known that at the time of Tamerlane the Great there was at Ak Shehir in Turkey a rus-

tic teacher-priest called Nasr-ed-Din Hodja
who had a talent for being very foolish as he
did wise things and being very wise as he did
foolish things. Even at his grave, the people
laugh, for his is no ordinary grave. It stands
on a hill near Ak Shehir. It is marked by a
single iron gate, carefully locked, but without
accompanying walls.

Nasr-ed-Din Hodja is as Turkish as Paul
Bunyan is American, but the Hodja carries
the accumulated humor of five centuries instead of one. Anyone who would really know
the Turk in his jovial mood can learn what
he is like by laughing with him at his best-
loved figure, Nasr-ed-Din Hodja.

CONTENTS

ILLUSTRATIONS

ONCE THE HODJA

HOW MANY DONKEYS?

THERE was the tinkle of tiny bells, the sharp clip of small hoofs, the throaty drone of a solitary singer. Nasr-ed-Din Hodja was bringing the donkeys back from the mill, their saddlebags filled with freshly ground wheat. The hot Turkish sun beat down on his turbaned head. The brown dust from the donkeys' hoofs puffed about him. The staccato trot of his donkey jiggled him back and forth. But Nasr-ed-Din Hodja was too pleased to be uncomfortable.

"I'll show them," he chuckled. "They gave me plenty of advice about taking care of their donkeys and their wheat. As though I did not know more about donkeys than any man in Ak Shehir."

His eyes rested lazily on the road ahead. At first it followed the brook running away from Mill Valley, the brook that turned the heavy stones to grind the wheat. Then the road disappeared over a hilltop.

"Just over that hill," he mused contentedly, "is Ak Shehir, where they are waiting for their donkeys. There is not a scratch or a bruise on one of the little creatures. No donkeys in all Turkey have had better treatment today than these nine."

Idly he began counting them.

"What?" he gasped. "Eight donkeys?"

He jumped from his donkey and ran hither and yon, looking behind rocks and over hilltops, but no stray donkey could he see. At last he stood beside the donkeys and counted again. This time there were nine. With a sigh of relief he climbed onto his own donkey and went singing along the road. His long legs in their baggy pantaloons swung easily back and forth in time to the donkey's trot.

Passing through a cluster of trees he thought it time to count the donkeys again.

"One—two—three—" and up to eight he counted, but no ninth donkey was to be seen. Down from his donkey's back he came. Behind all the trees he peered. Not a hair of a donkey could he find.

Again he counted, standing beside his donkeys. There they all were—nine mild little donkeys waiting for orders to move on. Nasr-ed-Din Hodja scratched his poor head in bewilderment. Was he losing his mind or were the donkeys all bewitched? Again he counted. Yes, surely there were nine.

"Ughr-r-r-r," Nasr-ed-Din Hodja gave the low guttural which is Turkish for "Giddap." As he rode on, he looked about him for the evil spirits which must be playing tricks on him. Each donkey wore the blue beads which should drive away the evil spirits. Were there evil spirits abroad stronger even than the blue beads?

He was glad to see a friend coming toward him down the road.

"Oh, Mustapha Effendi," he cried. "Have you seen one of these donkeys? I have lost a donkey and yet I have not lost it."

"What can you mean, Hodja Effendi?" asked Mustapha.

"I left the mill with nine donkeys," explained the Hodja. "Part of the way home there have been nine and part of the way there have been eight. Oh, I am bewitched! Help me! Help me!"

Mustapha was used to the queer ways of

the Hodja, but he was surprised. He counted the donkeys silently.

"Let me see you count the donkeys," he ordered the Hodja.

"One—two—three," began the Hodja, pointing at each one as he counted up to eight.

As he said the last number, he stopped and looked at his friend with a face full of help-lessness and terror. His terror turned to amazement as Mustapha slapped his knee and laughed until he almost fell from his donkey.

"What is so funny?" asked the Hodja.

"Oh, Hodja Effendi!" Mustapha laughed. "When you are counting your brothers, why, oh why, do you not count the brother on whom you are riding?"

Nasr-ed-Din Hodja was silent for a moment to think through this discovery. Then he kissed the hand of his deliverer, pressed it to his forehead and thanked him a thousand times for his help. He rode, singing, on to Ak Shehir to deliver the donkeys to their owners.

FOUR ARROWS

WHENEVER Tamerlane the Great was bored with his bowing courtiers and their everlasting, "Yes, my lord," he found relief in the companionship of Nasr-ed-Din Hodja. Here was a man who treated peasant and emperor alike. Here was a man who did not weigh every word before he let it reach his emperor's ears. Being with the Hodja was to Tamerlane like a fresh breeze from the mountains.

It was a sunny spring day when Tamerlane asked Nasr-ed-Din Hodja to go with him to the plain, where his soldiers were at their archery practice. The Hodja had been planning to plant onions that day, but he needed no urging to put off that back-breaking job till another day.

It was the sort of vivid, bracing day when a man feels twice as strong and clever as on a drab day. With each step across the fields to the place where the soldiers were practicing, Nasr-ed-Din Hodja felt younger and braver and more bursting with all sorts of skills. By the time they joined the soldiers, he was no longer the old man at whom all Ak Shehir loved to laugh. He was Tamerlane's fearless companion, a man who could do anything.

"A good shot that," said the Hodja as a soldier's arrow pierced the bull's-eye of the target. "It reminds me of the way I used to handle a bow and arrow."

"Really?" Tamerlane looked at the Hodja in surprise. "I had never heard that you were an archer."

"Oh, yes, indeed! I was a famous archer." On a day like this the Hodja could be anything. "I remember how men used to come from distant cities to see me shoot. My hands itch for the feel of the bow again."

No sooner was that wish out of the Hodja's mouth than Tamerlane beckoned to a soldier. "My soldiers need to see some good shooting," he said as he took the bow and arrow from the man. "Here is your chance to show us how it really should be done." Tamerlane held the bow and arrow toward the dumbfounded Nasr-ed-Din Hodja.

"Oh, you must not rob your soldier of his chance to practice." The Hodja was thinking faster than he had thought in many months. "He needs it so much more than I do."

"Watching your skill will more than make up for the time he loses." Tamerlane still held the bow and arrow toward the squirming Hodja.

"It is so long since I have worked at archery," hedged Nasr-ed-Din Hodja. "It might be better not to do it today."

"Oh, it will come back to you as soon as you feel the good strong bow in your hands." Tamerlane set the arrow in place, pulled back the bowstring, and sent the arrow whizzing within two hairs of the bull's-eye. "See! It is months since I have touched bow and arrow, but I feel as though I had been shooting yesterday."

"Perhaps I should wait until this cut on my finger heals." The Hodja tried to shift the interest from archery to a little scratch on one finger.

"That finger does not have to touch either bow or arrow," persisted Tamerlane.

"You forget the pain in my shoulder which has been bothering me all winter," mused the Hodja, grasping for anything to keep that bow and arrow out of his hands.

"You said this morning that today's spring sunshine had baked out that pain." Tamerlane held the bow and a fresh arrow firmly toward the Hodja.

Nasr-ed-Din Hodja knew a command when he saw it — and a command from Tamerlane was a command indeed.

A command from Tamerlane was a command indeed

"Oh, of course!" The Hodja tried to conjure up a jaunty air as he took the big bow in his awkward hands. A quick glance at a soldier at target practice showed him which way to hold it. After two or three tries he had the arrow fitted into somewhat near the right position. He squinted painfully at the target, pulled back the bowstring, and shut his eyes as the arrow wabbled limply to the ground just a few inches from his feet.

Tamerlane expected to see the Hodja angry or embarrassed. Not at all! The old jaunty grin suddenly spread over his face.

"That," said the Hodja, "is to show you how your Chief Huntsman shoots."

Nasr-ed-Din Hodja took another arrow from the soldier's quiver. He beamed pleasantly at the little group of soldiers that was fast gathering about him and Tamerlane. He put his arrow in place, gave a mighty pull on the string and sent the arrow whizzing high into the air. Half a dozen soldiers jumped

aside so that it hit no one as it fell to the
ground not far from its starting place.

"And that," said the Hodja with a cheerful
nod, "is to show you how your Governor
shoots."

Nasr-ed-Din Hodja took a third arrow and
adjusted it. The soldiers drew back ready to
dodge in any direction. It was well that they

did for the third arrow went far to the right of the mark.

"And that," said the Hodja genially, "is to show you how your General shoots."

Nasr-ed-Din Hodja took a fourth arrow. He no longer bothered to squint at the target. He merely put the arrow to the bowstring, gave a yank, and let it go where it would. This time the arrow left his bow with a businesslike buzz, whirred straight between the rows of grinning soldiers, and lodged neatly in the exact center of the bull's-eye.

For a minute, the Hodja stared with open mouth and popping eyes at his arrow quivering in the bull's-eye. "Mash Allah!" he muttered. "Mash Allah!" Then his old poise came back.

"And that," said he, as unconcerned as you please, "is to show you how Nasr-ed-Din Hodja shoots."

ONE CANDLE POWER

PERHAPS Nasr-ed-Din Hodja had been sitting too long in the warm coffee house, swapping yarns with his friends. The boasts were growing bigger and bigger. None was bigger than the Hodja's.

"I could stand all night in the snow without any fire to warm me." The Hodja noisily gulped down one more hot cup of sweet black coffee.

"No one could do that!" One of the men shivered as he looked through the window at the falling snow.

"I could!" The Hodja spread his hands over the open pan of burning coals. "I'll do it this very night."

"You can't!"

"I will! If I have so much as a glow of fire to warm myself, I'll — I'll — I'll give a feast for you all at my house tomorrow!"

The wager was on.

The friends of Nasr-ed-Din Hodja went home to their warm beds, while he stood alone in the snow-draped market square. He had never realized how much longer the hours were at night than in the daytime. He had never realized how many hours there were in the night. Once in a while a prowling dog or an adventuring cat would sniff at him and then slink off to a snugger spot. The cold snow swathing his feet and tickling his neck was hard enough to bear. Harder still was the sleepiness that plagued him. It would never do to fall asleep in the snow. He must keep awake to stamp his cold feet and beat his cold arms. He found that it was easier to fight off sleep if he fastened his eyes on the flickering candle in Mehmet Ali's house across the mar-

ket square. There was something cheering
about the wavering of that tiny flame, which
helped his tired eyes stay open.

Morning came at last. Curious men met
the shivering and yawning Hodja on his way
home to a cup of hot coffee. They asked about
his night and marveled at what he had done.

"How did you keep awake all night?" they
asked.

"I fixed my eyes on a flickering candle in
Mehmet Ali's house," he answered.

"A candle?"

"A burning candle?"

"Did you say a candle?"

"Of course!" The Hodja saw no harm in
watching a candle.

"A lighted candle gives flame. Flame gives
heat. You were warming yourself by the heat
of that candle. You have lost your wager."

At first the Hodja tried to laugh at their
joke, but he soon found that they were not
joking. For once, the Hodja was too tired to

argue successfully. Try as he would, he could not convince his friends that a candle in a distant house could give no warmth to a cold man standing in a snowy market square.

"What time shall we come for the feast at your house tonight?" The laughing men gathered about the Hodja, insisting that they had won the wager.

"Come at sunset," said the Hodja. He plodded drearily toward home. He was cold and very tired, but he was thinking — and thinking hard.

Just after the muezzin's musical voice sent the sunset call to prayer trilling over Ak Shehir, a group of men knocked at Nasr-ed-Din Hodja's street gate. It creaked open for them. They walked across the courtyard and left their shoes in a row beside the house door. They entered the Hodja's house and sat cross-legged on the floor.

"Dinner is not quite ready." It was the Hodja's voice from the kitchen.

"Oh, that's all right," called the men. "We are in no hurry."

They waited. There was an occasional footstep in the kitchen, but no sound of clattering dishes. They sniffed the air to guess what the feast might be, but they could smell no cooking food. They waited — and waited — and waited.

"I hope you are not hungry," called the

Hodja from the kitchen.   "Dinner is not quite ready yet."

"Perhaps we could help," suggested a hungry guest.

"Fine," called the Hodja.   "You might all come out in the kitchen to help."

The men, glad of anything to do, stretched their cramped legs.   As each man entered the kitchen, there passed over his face a look of surprise and then a sheepish grin.

There stood the Hodja earnestly stirring the contents of a big copper kettle which was suspended high in the air.   Far below it burned one flickering candle.

"Just a few minutes!"   The Hodja, standing a-tiptoe, peered into the cold kettle.   "It should boil before long.   A candle gives so much heat, you know!"

THREE FRIDAYS

THERE was just one day of each week that worried Nasr-ed-Din Hodja. On six days he was as free as a butterfly. He could talk with his friends in the market place or ride his donkey to a nearby village. He could work in the vineyards or go hunting in the hills. He could lounge in the coffee house or sit in the sun in his own courtyard. There was nothing to hurry him to be at a certain place at a certain time to do a certain thing.

But Friday was different. It was much different. That was the day when all good Mohammedans went to their mosques. Because Nasr-ed-Din Hodja, years before, had attended the school for priests, he was expected each Friday to mount the pulpit of the mosque at a certain time and preach a sermon. That was all very well when he had something to say, but there were many Fridays when his mind was as empty as that of his own little gray donkey. It was one thing to swap stories with the men in the coffee house and quite another to stand alone in the high pulpit and talk to a mosque full of people. The men, each squatting on his own prayer rug on the floor, looked up at him with such solemn faces. Then there was the fluttering in the balcony behind the lattices, which told him that the women were waiting too. Of course, the chanting, which came before the sermon, was not hard because all the men joined in that, bowing till they touched their foreheads to the floor in the Nemaz. But the sermon — that was hard.

One Friday he walked more slowly than ever through the cobblestoned streets of Ak Shehir. He saw the veiled women slipping silently past him on their way to the latticed balcony of the mosque. He saw the men in their best clothes hurrying to the mosque to hear his sermon. But what sermon? He stopped at the mosque door to leave his shoes. He pattered with the other men across the soft thick rugs. But they could squat on the rugs, while he had to climb into the high pulpit.

Perhaps the beauty of the mosque would give him an idea. He looked up at the blues and reds and whites of the intricate tracery on the ceiling, but not a thought came. He looked at the rich yellows and reds of the mosaics on the walls, but there was no help there. He looked at the men's faces staring up at him. He heard the tittering in the latticed balcony where the veiled women sat. He must say something.

"Oh, people of Ak Shehir!" He leaned on the pulpit and eyed them squarely. "Do you know what I am about to say to you?"

"No!" boomed from the rugs where the men squatted.

"No!" floated down in soft whispers from the latticed balcony, whispers not meant for any ears beyond the balcony.

"You do not know?" said Nasr-ed-Din Hodja, shaking his head and looking from one face to another. "You are sure you do not know? Then what use would it be to talk to people who know nothing at all about this

important subject. My words would be wasted on such ignorant people."

With that, the Hodja turned and climbed slowly down the pulpit steps. His eyes lowered, he walked with injured dignity through the crowds of men. He slipped on his shoes at the mosque door, and was out in the sunshine — free until next Friday.

That day came all too soon. The Hodja mingled with the crowds going to the mosque. His coarse, home-knit stockings pattered across the deep colorful rugs. He climbed the steps to the high pulpit. He looked down at the sea of solemn faces. He heard the rustling behind the lattices of the balcony. He had hoped that this week he could think of a sermon, but the carvings of the doorway did not help him, nor the embroidered hangings of the pulpit, nor the pigeons fluttering and cooing at the window. Still, he must say something.

"Oh, people of Ak Shehir!" intoned the

Hodja, gesturing with both hands. "Do you know what I am about to say to you?"

"Yes," boomed the men who remembered what had happened when they said "No" last week.

"Yes," echoed in soft whispers from the balcony.

"You know what I am going to say?" said the Hodja, shrugging first one shoulder and then the other. "You are sure you know what I am going to say? Then I need not say it. It would be a useless waste of my golden words if I told you something that you already knew."

The Hodja turned and again climbed down the pulpit steps. He picked his way with un-hurried dignity among the men. He scuffed into his shoes and escaped into the sunshine. Another free week was ahead of him.

But the best of weeks end. The third Friday found him once more climbing the pulpit steps, with not a word worth saying in that solemn mosque. The ancient Arabic writing on the bright ceiling had no help for him. The flickering candles in the large round chandelier winked at him but said nothing. Even the big Koran in front of him might have had blank pages instead of its fine Arabic words and its illuminated borders. Men's faces looked up at him expectantly. Bright eyes peered through the lattices of the women's balcony. The time had come again when he must speak.

"Oh, people of Ak Shehir!" declaimed the Hodja as he groped helplessly for an idea. "Do you know what I am about to say to you?"

"No," came from those who were thinking of the last Friday.

"Yes," came from those who were thinking of the Friday before that.

"Some of you know and some of you do not know!" The Hodja rubbed his hands together and beamed down at the men. "How very fine! Now let those who know tell those who do not know!"

The Hodja was humming to himself as he came down from the pulpit, two steps at a time. He nodded and smiled as he threaded his way through the men. Some thought he bowed and smiled toward the latticed balcony, but others said the good Hodja would not have made so bold. He picked his own worn shoes from the rows and rows by the mosque door. The sunshine was warm and friendly. The birds were singing and there was the fragrance of hawthorn blossoms in the air.

The Hodja had not a worry in the world — not till another Friday should come around.

A GUEST FOR HALIL

Hurry! You will be late for the banquet at Halil's house!" One person after another called this advice to Nasr-ed-Din Hodja as he jogged home from a day's work in his vineyard.

"They are right," the Hodja finally admitted. The sun was almost touching the horizon. "I will be late for the dinner, unless I go now — just as I am."

He turned his reluctant donkey's head about and was soon at Halil's house. He tied his donkey in Halil's courtyard and walked confidently into the house, where the feast was soon to begin. Always sure of a welcome, he spread his smiles and his jokes to right and to left. He was so happy talking that he did not notice for some time a very strange thing. He was talking to backs instead of to faces. Not a single man was listening to him! Soon an even stranger thing happened. When the soup was brought in, Halil ushered other men to seats at the low table, but he had no word for Nasr-ed-Din Hodja.

The Hodja cleared his throat noisily. Halil did not notice. He coughed loudly. Halil paid no attention.

"Oh, Halil Effendi!" called Nasr-ed-Din Hodja cheerily. "I noticed a fine crop of fruit in your vineyard today."

Halil, busy with his well-dressed guests, did not hear.

"Oh, Halil Effendi!" The Hodja's voice was even louder this time. "Your smallest grapes are twice as big as the best in my vineyard."

Still Halil seemed unable to hear or to see the one guest who stood alone in his shabby, dirty working clothes.

The Hodja looked thoughtfully at the other guests. Each man was scrubbed till he glistened. Each man was wearing his best clothes. Then the Hodja looked at his own brown hands, caked with the honest dirt of the vineyards. He looked at his own clothes with their patches upon patches, and with the day's new holes which the patient Fatima would mend that night.

Very quietly, Nasr-ed-Din Hodja slipped out of the door, untied his willing donkey and jogged home.

"Hot water, Fatima!" he ordered. "Soap, Fatima! My new shoes! My best turban! My new coat!"

Fatima bustled and fluttered about. Soon Nasr-ed-Din Hodja looked like a new man. He preened himself before the admiring Fatima, who had not seen her husband so completely well dressed in years. He strutted out of the house. Little boys spoke to him respectfully as he swaggered back along the

street to Halil's house.   Women peered from
behind their veils at the grand gentleman who
walked with such an air.

A bowing servant ushered him into the banquet room at Halil's house.   A beaming Halil
hurried to meet him and escort him to the best
seat in the room.   Men smiled and nodded.
Halil heaped his plate with goodies.   Questions and stories were directed toward Nasr-
ed-Din Hodja.

When he felt that all eyes were upon him,

the Hodja picked up the choicest piece of meat on his plate. He did not raise it to his lips. Instead, he opened his coat and placed it in a pocket which was hidden inside.

"Eat, coat, eat!" said the Hodja.

A handful of pilaf, a square of cheese, a pickle, and a fig followed the meat into the coat.

"Eat, coat, eat!" said the Hodja as he put in each tidbit. The guests stopped eating to watch the Hodja feed his coat.

Finally, Halil could hold in no longer. "Tell me, Hodja Effendi, what you mean by telling your coat to eat."

"Why, surely, you wish the coat to eat." The Hodja raised innocent eyes to Halil. "When I came in my old clothes, there was no place at the table for me. When I come in my new clothes, nothing is too good for me. That shows it was the coat, not me, that you invited to your banquet."

ARCHERY BY MOONLIGHT

EVER since the day that Nasr-ed-Din Hodja's arrow had surprised Tamerlane's soldiers by piercing the bull's-eye, he had kept a bow and arrow about the house, just in case it were needed. It made him feel safe to know that he was ready to defend his home and his wife no matter what threatened.

One night he was wakened by sounds in his yard. He lay in bed, trying to figure what it could be that went swishing and flapping under his window. Without waking his sleeping wife, he crept to the window, picking up his bow and arrow as he went. It was well to be prepared for anything.

It was a night when the moon was darting in and out among the clouds. When he first looked out of the window, his yard was in total blackness, but he could still hear a sound as of wind blowing through a thief's garments. It seemed to come from the corner of the yard under the old apricot tree, but not a thing could he see in the darkness. Suddenly from behind a cloud the moon popped out and the whole yard sprang into view. There was the rascal under the old apricot tree. The Hodja could see his coat swaying back and forth as he stood there, undecided where to start his thievery. Now was the time for Nasr-ed-Din Hodja to show himself a real hero.

He looked back at the sleeping Fatima and whispered, "Whatever fate may decree, your husband will protect you!   Sleep on unafraid! You are perfectly safe!"

He threw the window open wide, hoping the noise would send the thief running, but the moonlight showed the robed figure still standing uncertainly beneath the old apricot tree.

"Go away, thief!" shouted the Hodja. He waited. The figure under the apricot tree did not move.

"Go away, I say, or I will shoot you with my bow and arrow." This threat should have terrified the intruder. He did seem to tremble a little, but the brazen fellow held his ground.

"I am fitting an arrow to the bow," called the Hodja. Still the figure stood there. Fatima roused in her bed and mumbled sleepily.

"I am pulling back the bowstring," warned the Hodja, who wanted to give the poor fellow every chance to escape.

There stood the Hodja in the window, with the bowstring taut and the arrow in place. There stood the stubborn fellow under the apricot tree, ignoring every threat. Shooting a man was the last thing in the world the Hodja would care to do, but a threat was a threat and must be carried out. Suddenly the Hodja remembered that the only time he had hit the bull's-eye was the time he did not aim. This time he would aim carefully, and his arrow would hurt no one. He would be keeping his threat and would, without a doubt, frighten the man out of the yard.

"I shoot!" shouted the Hodja. He let the arrow fly.

Just then the moon hid behind another cloud and the yard was in blackness again. Strain his eyes as he would, not a thing could he see in the corner under the old apricot tree.

The thief was probably over the wall and running as fast as he could.

Feeling he had carried himself as a man should, the Hodja told the whole story, with gestures, to Fatima who was now three-quarters awake. Then he snuggled under his quilt and slept the sleep of the brave.

So sound was his sleep that he found Fatima was up and out-of-doors when he awoke in the morning. In fact, she had been up long enough to work herself into quite a rage. What could be the matter?

"Hodja Effendi! Hodja Effendi! Come here!" she called under his window. There was something in Fatima's voice which made the Hodja wish he were still asleep. What could he have done to displease her so? Well, he might as well face it now as later.

He stuck his head out of the window with, "What is it, my dear?"

Under his window he saw Fatima standing, holding up his own best coat which she had

In the back of the best coat stuck the arrow

washed the day before and hung to dry under the old apricot tree. In the back of the best coat stuck Nasr-ed-Din Hodja's arrow.

"You and your archery!" snorted Fatima, as she looked at the two jagged holes she would have to patch. Her scorn would have completely withered anyone less cheerful than Nasr-ed-Din Hodja.

"Oh, Allah be praised! Allah be praised!" sang the Hodja.

"Why praise Allah when you ruin your coat?"

"Oh, Fatima, don't you see that my life was saved as by a miracle?" cried the Hodja. "See where that arrow pierced the coat! Just think! If I had been inside the coat, the arrow would have gone clear through my stomach. Oh, Allah be praised! Allah be praised!"

THE RESCUE

NASR-ED-DIN HODJA yawned. He stretched his arms in their gaily striped sleeves. He stretched his long legs in their yellow pantaloons.

"Time for bed!" He rubbed his sleepy eyes. "But first a good cold drink of water."

Nasr-ed-Din Hodja reached for the earthen water jug. Empty!

"Fatima!" he called. "Fatima!"

No answer! He must go to the well and fill the jug himself.

Drowsily he stumbled to his feet. He straightened his turban which had fallen over one ear as he dozed. At the door he shoved his bare toes into his scuffly pointed shoes before he stepped out into the moonlit courtyard.

"Such an evening!" He breathed deeply of the cool night air.

As he ambled across to the well, Nasr-ed-Din Hodja was glad that Fatima had been asleep. It was worth the effort of coming out to the well just to see such a moon. He sniffed the fragrance of the almond blossoms, feathery soft in the silver light.

"I wonder if the water looks black or golden on a night like this," thought the Hodja. He leaned over to look down into the well. His drowsy eyes popped wide open.

Instantly he gave a low scream. "What has happened?" he cried. He looked wildly about for someone to help him.

"Fatima!" he called. "Fatima! The moon has fallen into the well!"

No answer! There was no one to help. Something had happened that would make the whole world a sadder, darker place. He, and only he, must make it right again. He would find a way. He would be a true hero.

Nasr-ed-Din Hodja fluttered about. He did not know exactly how to begin being a hero, but he did feel very brave and important.

"I have it!" he cried as he noticed the empty hook on the end of the rope he held in his hand. "If this hook can lift water jars in and out of the well, it surely can lift the moon out."

His hands trembling with excitement, he let the rope down deep into the well. The hook clattered on the rough stone sides as it went down. There was a muffled splash as it hit the water.

"Keep up your courage, good Moon!" The voice of the Hodja sounded hollow in the well. "I am here! All will soon be mended!"

He dangled the hook near the surface of the water, swinging it back and forth until he felt it catch on something solid. Giving never a thought to the jutting stones that lined the well, he was sure that it was the moon he had hooked.

He jerked and he tugged, but the hook held fast.

"Jump when I pull, good Moon," he called. "Do not pull against me."

He braced his feet and put every bit of strength into one mighty yank. Up came the hook. Down on the cobblestones of the court-yard went Nasr-ed-Din Hodja. He lay on his back, blinking up at the sky.

Suddenly he forgot the pain of his fall. He rubbed his eyes and looked again. Yes, there above him shone the full round moon. That mighty pull of his had carried the moon out of the well and had shot it back to its rightful place as queen of the night sky.

"Oh, Moon," said the Hodja in triumph, "it was a hard fight, but I saved you. Now you can shine again for all the world."

Rubbing his bruised head, he scuffled back into the house. He was so content with his own heroism that he completely forgot the empty water jug at the edge of the well.

A GIFT THAT CAME BACK

NASR-ED-DIN HODJA was sure that in
all the world there were no plums so sweet as
those that grew on his own plum trees. One
day he picked three of the largest, bluest plums
from his favorite tree. He put them on a copper tray, which he balanced carefully on his
head, and started for Tamerlane's house. He
was sure Tamerlane would think them the
sweetest plums he had ever tasted.

They proved, however, to be the most both-
ersome of plums. As Nasr-ed-Din Hodja
walked, they danced and they pranced on his
carefully balanced tray.

"Because you are up there where I cannot
see you," he scolded the plums, "you think
you can whirl like three dervishes."

Still the three plums jigged and reeled with each step the Hodja took.

"Stop dancing!" called the Hodja. "If you keep that up, I'll punish you by eating you."

Still the three plums twirled and cavorted.

There was nothing for the Hodja to do but to keep his promise. He sat down under a poplar tree and ate one plum — then another.

He spoke sternly to the third plum. "If I give you another chance, will you ride quietly on the tray?"

This lone plum seemed better behaved. It sat quite calmly in the middle of the tray on the Hodja's head for the rest of the journey.

Now it happened to be one of Tamerlane's jolly days. He received Nasr-ed-Din Hodja with the courtesy due an honored guest. Vowing he had never tasted a sweeter plum, he did not so much as hint that it seemed a lonely one. He laughed at the Hodja's jokes, calling for more and more of them. Finally, when the Hodja realized that he must hurry to be home before dark, Tamerlane filled his tray with gifts — gifts that proved easy to carry. Nasr-ed-Din Hodja reached home just at dusk, well pleased with his day.

That satisfied feeling stayed with him for a week. Then he decided it was time to call on Tamerlane again.

"What gift shall I take him?" he mused as he looked at the empty tray. The plums were past their prime now — too soft to stand the jogging journey.

"What about some good red beets?" thought the Hodja, still staring at the empty tray. "Yes, beets will be just the thing. They are so hard that they will not bruise, even if they do dance and prance on the tray."

Into his garden went the Hodja to pull some of his reddest, firmest beets. He heaped these on the tray, balanced the tray on his head, and swung off, humming happily, toward Tamerlane's house.

On the way he met his good friend Hassan.

"Where are you taking those fine beets, Hodja Effendi?" asked Hassan.

"These beets are a gift for Tamerlane."

"Beets — for — Tamerlane?" Hassan was doubtful.

"Aren't beets a good gift for Tamerlane?" The Hodja took the tray from his head and looked at the beets as though for the first time. They did not seem quite as magnificent as when he was pulling them. "Perhaps something else would be better?"

"Yes, something else."

"For instance?"

"Figs!" Hassan seemed very sure. "Juicy ripe figs just fresh from the tree."

"Yes, figs would be a much better gift." Nasr-ed-Din Hodja wondered why he had not thought of it before. He turned into the market where he traded his firm red beets for a tray of juicy ripe figs.

"You are lucky," the fig seller told him, "to get so many luscious figs for a few common

beets." However, the fig seller's next remark
was not for the Hodja's ears. "I am lucky to
get rid of those soft figs. They were so much
too ripe that I was just ready to throw them
away."

Pleased with his bargain, Nasr-ed-Din
Hodja went on to Tamerlane's court. Now,
it happened that this was not one of Tamerlane's jolly days. Instead, it was one of his
grumpy, sulky, pouting days. The Hodja's
cheerful grin and his tray of overripe figs were

more than he could stand. All day he had
been wanting someone to kick or to punch.
Here was his chance.

"Come at once!" he shouted to his servants.
Six of them came running.

"Take this man's figs and throw them at
him!" he shouted. "Throw every single one
of them at him! And throw them hard!"

The Hodja turned and ran, but the servants
and the figs followed him. Smack! Splash!
Squash! Spatter! Not a fig missed him. Not

a fig failed to pop open and spill its liquid on the fleeing Hodja. He looked as though he had been sprayed with seeds and green water.

Nasr-ed-Din Hodja was still running, as fast as his loose flopping shoes would let him, when he met Hassan.

"Oh, Hassan Effendi, let me thank you seven times below the earth for what you have done for me!"

Hassan stared at the bespattered Hodja.

"Oh, Hassan Effendi, I thank you seven times above the heavens for what you did for me!"

Hassan, who knew the ways of Tamerlane, began to realize what must have happened. "Why do you thank me?" he asked.

"Oh, it is good that I took your advice — your wise, wise advice."

"Why?" Hassan was still bewildered.

"If it had been the hard red beets that I gave to Tamerlane," explained Nasr-ed-Din Hodja, "if it had been the hard red beets that his servants threw at me —" He could not finish the sentence. He was thinking what a bruised and broken man he would have been. "Oh, Hassan Effendi, it is wise to take the advice of good friends. Allah be praised!"

THE BEAR IN THE PEAR TREE

THE ring of Nasr-ed-Din Hodja's axe sounded through the woods of the lonely mountainside. There was silence as the Hodja rested. It was very still on that mountainside — no noise but the twitter and call of birds, the hum and chirp of insects, and the rustle and whir of the leaves in the forest.

Suddenly the Hodja jumped to his feet. What was that tramping, crackle — crunch — crackle, through the twigs on the forest floor? That was not the footsteps of a squirrel, a rabbit, or a fox. Nasr-ed-Din Hodja stood frozen to attention, his eyes fixed on the place from which the sound came, crunch — crackle — crunch, steadily nearer and nearer, steadily louder and louder. A glimpse of moving black fur! Four stiff legs swinging awkwardly toward him! A shiny black nose between sharp eyes! The biggest bear the Hodja had seen in all his wood-chopping days!

For once the Hodja did not stop to argue. He ran for the nearest tree, a wild pear tree, and scrambled up it more nimbly than he had moved since he was a boy.

Crackle — crunch — crackle. Straight toward the pear tree, looking neither to right nor to left, plodded the enormous black bear. The nearer it came, the bigger it seemed. Crunch — crackle — crunch. It was directly under the very tree where the Hodja was hiding. The bear yawned. It stretched. It yawned again. It lay down on the ground under the pear tree, gave a drowsy grunt, and closed its eyes.

"You don't fool me that way!" thought the Hodja. "You pretend to sleep but you are just waiting to pounce on me." Nasr-ed-Din Hodja clung to the branch, his eyes fixed wildly on the big bear. He expected it any minute to jump at him. He wanted to climb higher in the tree, but was afraid of the telltale sounds he might make.

He saw the bear's muscles tighten. He thought of all the mistakes of his life — of all the times he had been cross to Fatima, of all the times he had played tricks on people. He looked down at his home valley, perhaps for the last time. Then the bear shivered. It relaxed. Its breathing lengthened into a loud snore.

"You are asleep!" whispered the Hodja, not quite sure that he dared believe what he saw. He wriggled about, trying to find a comfortable place on his high perch. A magpie scolded to find such a clumsy stranger in her favorite tree. An inquisitive bee buzzed about the Hodja. The bear below the tree snored cozily. The Hodja squirmed from one position to another, making little showers of leaves and twigs fall around the heavily sleeping bear.

From far down in the valley floated dimly

the musical chant of muezzins in many mina-
rets, singing forth thc call to prayer, "Allah
eekbar, Allah eekbar."

"That means that it is two hours till sunset," thought the Hodja, wondering how long
this could last.

Lower and lower marched the sun. Stiffer
and stiffer grew the Hodja's poor cramped
body. The sun touched the horizon and the
melodious call to prayer, "Allah eekbar, Allah
eekbar," wafted up from the valley.

The sun was down and the moon shining so
brightly that the Hodja could peer through
his leafy screen and see the huge black bulk
below him rise and fall regularly as the big
bear snored. Once more the lilting sweetness
of the call to prayer floated up from the vil-
lages in the valley.

"That means two hours after sunset!"
groaned the Hodja as he looked pleadingly
toward Mecca, the sacred city in the east.

At last there was a stirring in the black mass

below him. The big bear stretched, rose stiffly to his feet, and sniffed hungrily. Then, to the Hodja's horror, it stuck its great claws into the very pear tree where the Hodja was clinging. Up the tree it came, while the poor Hodja trembled so that he could scarcely hang onto the branches. Sniff went the great nose, until the bear found just what he wanted — a juicy wild pear. Eating and climbing, eating and climbing, up the tree came the bear. Shivering and shaking, shivering and shaking, up the tree went the Hodja. Finally, the Hodja was on the highest branch that could possibly hold his weight. Oh, if only the bear would be content to climb no higher! Smack, smack went the bear's great lips until every wild pear within reach was gone. Then up it went, so close that the Hodja could feel its hot breath. Out went one big paw, scooping up a pear, and swinging around so that it almost touched the Hodja's mouth. Was it trying to share the pears?

Up the tree came the bear

"Oh, no, thank you!" screamed the Hodja, trying to be polite even at such a time. "I do not care for pears. I never eat them. No, never, never, never!"

Now, the bear was really a gentle and shy old fellow, not at all prepared to have sudden screams pop out at it from behind a leafy branch. With a terrified howl, the bear lost its balance and toppled crashing through the branches. There was a thud as it hit the ground. Then there was silence — welcome silence.

The Hodja spent the rest of the night edging slowly down the tree, his eyes warily on the black heap that lay motionless in a patch of moonlight below him. After each move, the Hodja would wait to be sure that the bear still lay lifeless. By morning, the Hodja had reached the lowest branch of the wild pear tree. As the first rays of daylight shone through the woods, even the cautious Hodja

was certain that the bear would never frighten anyone again. Never again would it climb trees to eat wild pears in the moonlight.

Nasr-ed-Din Hodja jumped clumsily from the lowest branch, a million needles pricking his numb arms and legs. He started limping toward home and breakfast, thinking what a story he would have to tell. However, the more he pictured himself telling of his harrowing night, the more he felt there would not be much glory in the telling for him. Something was wrong with a story that showed him up to be so shaky a hero.

Suddenly his old grin burst over his tired face. He ran back to the pear tree, whipped out his knife, and skinned the big bear. With the thick black fur slung over his shoulders, he strode singing down the mountainside and across the plain toward Ak Shehir. He did not enter the city by the small gate nearest his home, but walked around the city wall to enter by the main gate near the market place. He did not take the shortest path through the market to his house, but walked through one busy street after another, until all Ak Shehir knew — or thought it knew — that Nasr-ed-Din Hodja was a mighty hunter.

He did not need to say a word about his experiences of the night. Other people were talking for him, talking about the brave and wonderful Hodja who had killed the huge and ferocious black bear, single-handed.

THE DONKEY GOES TO MARKET

I TELL you, no! I will not keep this miserable donkey another day!" Nasr-ed-Din Hodja glared at the little gray donkey that was patiently switching off the myriad flies as it waited for the Hodja to fasten on the piece of old rug that served as a saddle.

"A new donkey might be just as stubborn," suggested Fatima.

"This wretch is more than stubborn!" stormed the Hodja. "It eats like an elephant but grows skinnier every day. It is slow as a tortoise, lazy as a pig, mean as a fox, stupid as a fish, and stubborn as a — as a — as a donkey!"

Fatima patted the little donkey who rubbed its head affectionately against her striped sleeve. Fatima said nothing. She had argued with her husband enough times to know that it was like throwing dry leaves on a fire.

"Say your good-byes to the creature!" Nasr-ed-Din Hodja threw one long leg over the little animal. He made the low throaty "Ughr-r-r-r," which is marching orders to a Turkish donkey. "Next time you see it, someone else will be riding it. You shall see what a fine donkey I shall ride home from the animal market. You know how good I am at buying and selling. I can sell this wretched donkey for enough to buy a fine one, and still have a gold piece left over for you to sew in your headdress."

"Ughr-r-r-r," he whirred to the donkey again. The little animal reluctantly shook its long ears, picked up one tiny hoof, and was off. Gloating over the great bargain he was to strike in the market that day, the Hodja patted the coarse hair of his donkey's neck.

Through the street gate rode the Hodja,

and on toward the market place. His long legs dangled at the donkey's sides, his feet sometimes touching the cobblestones of the narrow street. It was hard to pass by the charms of market day, but the Hodja had important business on hand. He nodded to right and to left at his many friends in the market place, but kept straight on until he reached the animal market.

"Here is a donkey that will make some man proud of his bargain," said the Hodja as he handed the donkey over to the auctioneer.

"Such a good donkey should bring a good price," said the auctioneer. He poked the donkey, pinched its legs, and looked at its teeth. Like the Hodja, he spoke loudly for the benefit of anyone who might be listening.

One after another, the auctioneer led the animals up for sale but not a bid did the Hodja make. His eyes were fixed on one donkey that was bigger, sleeker, and plumper than the others. Surely that was the donkey for him.

Finally, all the donkeys were sold but two —
the one Nasr-ed-Din Hodja had brought and
the one he had resolved to ride away. He was
relieved to see that the auctioneer led up his
old donkey first. It would be good to have
the money for his sale jingling in his belt with
what money he already had before he started
bidding for the beautiful dark donkey on
which he had set his heart.

"Here is a donkey worth buying!" The
auctioneer rubbed his hands gloatingly as he
set the Hodja's old donkey before the little
group of buyers. "I have watched this donkey many a time and wished it was mine. See
that wise look in its eyes! See the gentle way
it holds its head! One look at this donkey
shows that it would obey your orders before
you gave them!"

Nasr-ed-Din Hodja looked at the donkey's
eyes. There was a wise look he had never
noticed.

"And look at the muscles," the auctioneer

droned on. "What loads it could carry! What hills it could climb! Those slim legs mean speed. I wager this donkey could run faster than any donkey in Ak Shehir!"

The Hodja looked at the donkey's legs. He had never noticed how strong and slim they were.

"See how smooth this donkey's coat is!" said the auctioneer. "That shows good care. What a pretty shade of gray! What perfectly matching white boots on its feet!"

The Hodja squinted thoughtfully at the donkey. It was prettily marked. Strange he had never noticed.

"How much am I offered for the handsomest, strongest, wisest, gentlest, most industrious donkey in all Ak Shehir?"

"Fifty ghurush," offered a villager.

Nasr-ed-Din Hodja glared at him. Fifty ghurush for the finest donkey in Ak Shehir, indeed!

"Two liras," called the Hodja.

"Two and a half liras," called a villager.

"Three!" The Hodja held up three fingers.

"Four!"

"Five!"

"Six!"

Up and up went the price until a villager bid ten liras.

"Wait a minute!" called the excited Hodja. He grabbed his money bag from his belt and

counted his money.   Just what he thought!
Ten liras and eleven ghurush.

"Ten liras and five ghurush," called a villager.

"Ten liras and eleven ghurush," shouted
the Hodja.

He waited.   Silence!

"Only ten liras and eleven ghurush for this
wonderful donkey!" exclaimed the auctioneer
who knew perfectly well that was a good price.
"Come, someone!   Make it eleven liras."

Everyone waited.   Silence!

The auctioneer handed the bridle to Nasr-
ed-Din Hodja.   The Hodja emptied his
money bag into the auctioneer's hand.   He
threw his long legs over the donkey's back and
settled into the familiar saddle.

"Ughr-r-r," he whirred to the donkey and
off they trotted toward home.   How proud of
his bargaining Fatima would be!

Halfway home he began wondering why he
had an empty money bag.   He had planned,

by good bargaining, to bring home a donkey and more money than he carried away.   It was puzzling.   Perhaps Fatima could explain. And perhaps she did.

ONE LAST PICNIC

IN HIS huge yellow turban, with his black coat thrown open over his striped blouse and baggy trousers, Nasr-ed-Din Hodja made a bright spot against the mud-brick walls of Ak Shehir. He stood watching the cloud of brown dust rolling along the road that led from the hillside pastures. He hummed the same plaintive tune that the shepherd boy was playing on his wooden flute, a tune that moaned shrill and monotonous above the bleating and baaing of the sheep and goats, above the quick thud of their many hoofs.

"Can you pick out your own sheep from the flock?" Ahmet had just joined Nasr-ed-Din Hodja and leaned lazily against the mud-brick wall beside him.

"Mine is probably the leader!" The Hodja did not realize that his pride in his lone sheep was the joke of all Ak Shehir. He raised his hand to shade his eyes from the setting sun, the better to identify his precious sheep. "Isn't the leader the plumpest and the whitest of them all?"

"If the best animal leads, it must be yours!" There was fun in Ahmet's eye that the Hodja missed. The flocks were now near enough that the men could distinguish the individual sheep.

"Oh, my old eyes must be failing me," said the Hodja. "The leader is a most ordinary sheep. But do you see that one in the middle of the flock? See how long and curly its wool is! See how white it shines in the light of the setting sun! See how plump it is! That is my sheep."

Nasr-ed-Din Hodja shuffled forward and claimed his sheep. He sank one hand caressingly in his pet's thick wool and walked beside it toward home. Ahmet matched his stride to the shorter step of the older man. He had no sheep or goat of his own to lead home.

"That is a fine sheep, Hodja Effendi," mused Ahmet. "How plump! How tender! Mash Allah!"

Nasr-ed-Din Hodja cast a suspicious glance at Ahmet who went on as though thinking aloud, "What a shame to have so choice a sheep wasted when the end of the world comes tomorrow!"

"The end of the world?" Nasr-ed-Din Hodja stared at Ahmet.

"Of course. Hadn't you heard?" Ahmet did not look the Hodja directly in the eye. "If we roasted the sheep soon enough, it would not be wasted when the end of the world comes tomorrow. Oh, well! Of course you would not want to do that!"

"No, of course not!" They had now reached Nasr-ed-Din Hodja's gate but the two men lingered while the Hodja asked, "What makes you think the end of the world is coming tomorrow?"

"Why, haven't you heard? Everyone is talking about it." Ahmet turned to call to a group of men who were sitting in the fading sunlight by the next gate. "Nasr-ed-Din Hodja has not heard that the end of the world is coming. He does not realize how wise it would be to save this plump sheep by eating it while we are alive to enjoy it."

"Oh, that would be the only sensible thing to do," agreed the men, with as gloomy faces as they could manage.

Nasr-ed-Din Hodja looked at his fat sheep, waiting patiently for the gate to open and let it into its own courtyard. He looked at the men who were talking so wisely about the end of the world that was coming tomorrow, when sheep, no matter how plump and tender, would be of no use to anyone.

Then the Hodja made his great decision.

"Meet me at the river bank tomorrow morning," said he. "We'll have a fine meal of roast mutton."

With great effort the men kept from laughing until the Hodja was safely inside his own courtyard, with the gate shut behind him.

The next day was warm and clear, a perfect day for a picnic at the river's edge. The men invited by Nasr-ed-Din Hodja and many of their friends were there when the first curls of smoke rose from the fire on which the Hodja was to roast the mutton and cook a huge kettle of pilaf — rice pilaf with pistachio nuts.

"Our last day in the world," the Hodja was droning. Were the tears he was wiping from his eyes caused by sorrow or by the smoke from the wood fire? "Our last day in this world. Praise be to Allah that it is warm and sunny. If I were not busy roasting this mutton, I would go for one last swim in the river, the cool green river that has comforted us so many years but is so soon to stop flowing."

"A good idea," agreed the men. "We can

go for a swim while you roast the meat."

In no time at all their clothes were in a heap beside the busy Hodja and they were splashing in the river. They could not, through the bushes that hemmed the river, see the Hodja, but they could hear the crackle of the fire and the drone of his voice. "Any minute now the end of the world may come. It may be this hour. It may be the next. The end of the world — the end of the world — "

Hearing him moan on about the fate that was ahead, his splashing friends were almost ashamed of their trick. They agreed that, while they were dressing, they would tell him that it was all a prank. Then they could laugh about it together while they ate the feast which their jest had won for them. They hoped he would see what a side-splitting joke it really was.

The aroma of the roasting mutton, mixed

with a less pleasant smell which they could not identify, was soon more than the hungry men could endure. They climbed, blowing and spraying, out of the river, pushed their way through the scratchy bushes and stood beside Nasr-ed-Din Hodja. They stared, big-eyed, at the grassy bank where they had thrown their clothes.

It was as green and empty as it had been when the sun rose that morning. On the fire, burning smudgily, were their clothes. The men stared, open-mouthed but mute, first at the Hodja and then at the charring mass which had once been shoes and coats and pantaloons.

The Hodja beamed at them, his smile altogether amiable and guileless. "Oh, about your clothes!" he chirped. "I was cleaning up around here and I realized that, with the end of the world coming in just a few minutes, you would never be needing them again."

PUMPKIN TREES AND WALNUT VINES

"OH, HOW hot my poor head is!" Nasred-Din Hodja sat alone under a walnut tree. He fanned himself with a pumpkin leaf that he had picked from the vine sprawling at his feet.

"I wonder if I dare take off this hot turban." The Hodja looked to the right, to the left, behind him, before him. "There's not a soul in sight. And for once, I can take off my turban without anyone laughing at my baldness!"

He unwound his turban and wiped his dripping hot head with it. He threw the turban down on the ground beside him, and he sighed contentedly as the breeze from the pumpkin-leaf fan blew on his smooth glistening head.

"There, I feel like myself," said the Hodja, comfortable and contented again. "That was a good day's work I did in the vineyard today. I have earned a good supper. Fatima said she was going to cook goat's-milk soup for supper. I'll just rest here a minute to cool off, then go home to a good big bowl to fill me up."

With the sense of well-being, the Hodja always felt the urge to talk to someone — to tell of his exploits or to give advice. But he had already made sure that not a soul was in sight. He could hear the tinkle of sheep bells and the reedy whine of a shepherd's flute on the distant hillside, but not a person could he see.

The pumpkin-leaf fan waved more slowly, as Nasr-ed-Din Hodja sat erect. The fan dropped to the ground. The Hodja was wide awake again. He had discovered something that really should be changed.

"You silly old tree!" Nasr-ed-Din Hodja shook an accusing finger at the walnut tree that was shielding him. "Is that the best you

can do? And that? And that?" The Hodja
pointed scornfully at the walnuts growing on
the tree.

"Look at the size of you!" The Hodja
shook his fist at the tree. He was working up
a pleasant excitement. "You rise up so proud
and high, but what do you have to brag about
— just some little walnuts no bigger than my
two thumbs. Take a lesson from your neighbor, the pumpkin vine. It lies along the
ground, feeling so humble and unimportant,

but see what good reason it has to brag." The Hodja pointed at the huge golden pumpkins, snuggled among the dark green leaves of the pumpkin vine.

The more he thought about it, the more disgusted the Hodja became with a scheme of things which made little walnuts grow on a noble tree and huge pumpkins grow on a groveling vine.

"Now, if I had been planning it," cried the Hodja to his audience of walnuts and pumpkins, "it would have been very different! The big important pumpkins would be waving proudly on the strong branches of this big important tree. The little unimportant walnuts could cling without any trouble to the spineless pumpkin vine. The vine might even hold up its head a little, if it had something the right size growing on it."

Unnoticed by him, a gentle breeze had sprung up and was swaying the branches above his bald bare head.

He rubbed his poor head

"Yes, yes," he went on, "if I had been planning the trees and the vines, you—"

The Hodja never finished his sentence. There was a little snap on the branch above his head. There was a little crackle as something rushed through the leaves. There was a resounding smack as something hit the Hodja's bald bare head.

For a minute the Hodja swayed. He saw little bright lights where none had been before. With his left hand he picked up a walnut, small, to be sure, but hard, oh, very hard. With his right hand he rubbed his poor head where a lump the size of a walnut was quickly rising.

The Hodja bowed apologetically toward the sacred city of Mecca in the east.

"Oh, Allah!" It was a meek and humble Hodja who spoke. "Forgive me for saying you were wrong to have pumpkins grow on vines and walnuts grow on trees. You were wiser than I. Suppose it had been a pumpkin that fell from that tree onto my poor head!"

Rubbing his bruised and aching head, the Hodja sat under the walnut tree. He was thinking how beautiful the golden pumpkins looked on their graceful twining vine. They were so close to the good brown earth that they could not possibly fall anywhere. Allah was wise. Allah be praised.

THAT OTHER LEG

NASR-ED-DIN HODJA was striding through the streets, one hand firmly grasping the roast goose tucked under his arm, the other hand pinching his own nose tight shut. He could not trust himself to let the fragrance of the roast goose tempt him. The goose was a present for Tamerlane and must arrive without nibbles breaking its crunchy goodness.

A fly lighted on the Hodja's forehead. He took his hand from his nose just long enough to brush the fly away, but even that moment was too long. The spicy aroma of the roast goose sank deep into his nostrils. He remembered what a long time it was since he drank his morning cup of coffee; how much longer it had been since he last tasted good roast goose. After all, there was plenty to eat in the palace.

Tamerlane would never miss a little portion of the goose, a plump crisp leg for instance.

Nasr-ed-Din Hodja walked on toward Tamerlane's palace, nibbling a leg of the roast goose. As he walked through the palace yard, he could not help wondering what Tamerlane would think of a roast goose with but one leg. Never mind! He would worry about that when the time came. The good leg he had eaten was worth any trouble that might come because it was gone.

Nasr-ed-Din Hodja found Tamerlane quite by himself and glad of company. The great ruler seemed as thankful for the succulent goose as though his huge pantry shelves were empty.

He turned the goose over and over the better to admire its rich fatness.

"What a cook your Fatima is!" exclaimed Tamerlane. "No one in my kitchen can roast a goose to such perfection!"

"Yes, Fatima is a fine cook," agreed the

Hodja.   He chattered on as fast as he could about Fatima's pilafs, Fatima's soups, Fatima's dolmas, Fatima's baklava.   If he talked fast enough, the absence of the leg might not be noticed.

"Hm-m-m-m!   This   is   strange — very strange!"   Tamerlane was looking at the leg-less side of the goose.   "This goose has only one leg!"

"To be sure!" The Hodja looked out of the window, playing for time to think what to say. "To be sure! How many legs would you expect?"

"Two legs, of course!"

"Two legs?" The Hodja laughed, his eyes alight at something he had seen through the open window. "Not at Ak Shehir. Geese in other towns may have two legs, or three, or four for all I know, but the geese of Ak Shehir are famous for being one-legged."

"How can you lie to me like that?" Tamerlane jumped to his feet, his good-natured mood as gone as the goose's leg. "You know as well as I do what happened to that other leg. One-legged geese of Ak Shehir, indeed!"

"Well, if you won't take my word for it, look with your own eyes." Nasr-ed-Din Hodja pointed out of the window. "There is a flock of Ak Shehir's famous one-legged geese by your own fountain."

Tamerlane looked where the Hodja pointed.

By the fountain — could he believe it? — he saw a dozen big white geese sleeping in the sun, each goose supporting itself steadily on one slim yellow leg.

"How many legs do you see?" asked the Hodja. "I count twelve geese and twelve legs. Can you count any more than twelve?"

Tamerlane stared and clicked his tongue. "No."

Funny he had never noticed before. What with waging wars and setting up a new government, he had been far too busy to notice geese.

"The geese of my boyhood village in Asia had two legs apiece, I am sure." Tamerlane's voice was apologetic.

"That's perfectly possible," agreed the Hodja kindly. "But this is not your boyhood village. This is Ak Shehir, the home of one-legged geese."

"I've been too busy to *notice such things*," murmured Tamerlane.

"Well, I must be going," said the Hodja with an anxious glance at the sleeping geese. "Selamun aleykum!"

"Ve aleykum —" began Tamerlane, but he never finished his farewell.

Just at that moment, a camel that had been sleeping beside the fountain stretched itself and squealed with all the power of its long, strong neck. Its voice ran up and down the scale, shrilling and screaming. It echoed and re-echoed in the walled courtyard. With a hiss, the twelve geese woke from their sleep. With a louder hiss, each stretched out the leg that had been tucked under its wing. With a great flapping and hissing, the twelve geese scattered, each goose running on two perfectly good legs.

By the time Tamerlane came to his senses, Nasr-ed-Din Hodja was down in the courtyard below his window. Quite forgetting his dignity, Tamerlane stuck his royal head out of the window. He called after the Hodja some-

thing that sounded more like the hiss of a
goose mixed with the squeal of a camel than
it sounded like the words of a great conqueror
who had just accepted a gift from a loyal subject.   But the Hodja was ready with his answer.

"My good Tamerlane," called the Hodja
just before the palace gate opened for him,
"if you or I had such a racket poured into our
ears when we were asleep, we would each
sprout at least four legs!"

And Tamerlane, in spite of himself, smiled
as he pulled off the remaining leg of the goose
and sank his teeth in its tenderness.

FOUR BRAYS OF A DONKEY

"CLING-CLANG," rang the axe of Nasr-ed-Din Hodja, high in the mulberry tree. The Hodja was sitting astride a limb, his long black coat rolled to his waist, and his legs, in their baggy yellow pantaloons, swinging back and forth in time to his chopping.

"Khayr olsoun, Hodja Effendi!" called a voice from below.

"Khayr olsoun, Halil Effendi!" The Hodja leisurely shifted his balance on the limb. Resting on his axe, he arranged his turban which had twisted awry.

"You are going to fall out of that tree!" warned Halil.

The Hodja grinned. He was good-natured but unconcerned.

"But you really will," pleaded Halil. "Look where you are sitting!"

"You better look where you are walking!" countered the Hodja. "People who walk along looking into the treetops and clouds are sure to stub their toes."

"But look where you are chopping!" begged Halil.

"Cling-clang," sounded the axe of Nasr-ed-Din Hodja.

"You better look where you are — " began the Hodja. But he never told Halil where to look.

Crash! Down came the limb. Down came the axe. Down came Nasr-ed-Din Hodja. He had been too busy and too stubborn to notice on which side of the cutting he had been sitting.

After the first groans and the first rubbing of bruises, the Hodja had a sudden thought.

"You are a wise man, Halil Effendi," the Hodja said. "You told me when I was going to fall. You are a prophet and the son of a prophet. Tell me, now, when I am going to die."

"After your donkey brays four times," said Halil. He was so disgusted with the simple old Hodja that he thought any answer would do.

Too bruised and shaken to work any more, the Hodja swung his leg over his little gray donkey's back and started for home.

After they had gone a little distance, the donkey thought

of the manger of hay and of its baby donkey
at home. It stretched out its neck and brayed.
Suddenly the Hodja remembered Halil's
prophecy. Halil had been right about the
fall from the mulberry tree. He must be a
true prophet.

"Aman, aman!" shivered the Hodja as the
bray shattered the stillness. "I am one fourth
dead!"

A bit farther on the road, they met another
donkey and rider. The Hodja's little animal
brayed a friendly greeting.

"Vai, vai!" shuddered the Hodja. "I am
one half dead!"

On they jogged. The donkey began thinking of the brook where it would soon be
drinking. It had been a hot day and the water
would taste cool and good. It let out a bray
of anticipation. The Hodja tried to muffle
that third bray, but the bray of a donkey is not
to be muffled.

"Aman, aman!" The Hodja's groans were

like a dirge as the bray shook him. "I am now three fourths dead!"

Unhappily, like a cat who has lost eight of its nine lives, the doomed Hodja rode on. He patted the donkey and chatted to it to divert the little animal from another bray. He thought of the years ahead when he would have to anticipate the donkey's every want to keep it from giving that last fatal bray. He wondered if there was any way to cut out a donkey's bray without hurting the little beast of whom he was so fond. He must ask Halil about this. Halil was a prophet and the son of a prophet. He knew everything.

There were voices ahead, the voices of men shouting orders to their donkeys. The ears of Nasr-ed-Din Hodja's friendly little donkey pricked forward. It sniffed. It must let its donkey friends know it was coming. Loud and long was the donkey's bray of greeting. It was the fourth bray of the donkey.

"Aman, aman!" screamed the Hodja as he

toppled from his donkey. "I am dead! I am dead!"

The men of the approaching caravan rushed forward. They picked up the limp Hodja. They shook him. They shouted at him. They poked him. They pinched him. He was as limp as an empty saddlebag.

"He said he was dead," argued the men. "Surely he must know."

"We must take him to his own village," said they.

They loaded the limp body of the Hodja onto his own donkey. With his long striped girdle they bound him to the donkey's saddle. They turned back toward Ak Shehir discussing how to break the sad news to Fatima.

On their way, they came to a path which seemed to be a short cut to the village.

"The short cut is too muddy," said one of the men.

"But the longer road is too rocky," said another.

"The short road saves an hour's journey," said a third.

"There is a cool spring by the long road," said a fourth.

On and on they argued, until —

"When I was alive," began Nasr-ed-Din Hodja.

The men stared with open-mouthed wonder and fear. The Hodja was sitting up on his donkey's back, quite unable to keep out of a good argument.

"When I was alive, we always went this way." The Hodja pointed to the shorter path. The men shouted at their donkeys and disappeared in a rapid thud of small hoofs.

Home again by the short cut, Nasr-ed-Din Hodja sat long over the warmth in his mongal, pondering. Dead or alive — which was he?

THREE QUESTIONS

A LETTER for you, Nasr-ed-Din Hodja Effendi!" The Mayor's messenger beamed as he handed a piece of paper to the surprised Hodja.

"A letter? For me?" The Hodja stared at the paper and turned it over and over in his hand. A letter did not come every day in those times when few people knew how to read and write. Luckily, the Hodja was one of the learned ones. He could spell out words and write some of them.

"Well, read it!" came from behind the veil Fatima had hastily dropped before her face as the messenger approached.

"Yes, read it!" urged the messenger, who had been regretting his lack of education all the time he carried the letter he could not read.

The Hodja cleared his throat, pulled himself to his tallest, and read:

"Three traveling priests, very learned men, are visiting in Ak Shehir. They have questions to ask of our wisest men. Will you come to a feast in honor of the priests that they may ask you questions? Come at once."

Now what could be more fun than a feast and a conversation with learned strangers all on the same day? Not waiting even to brush the dust from his coat, the Hodja saddled his donkey and was off so fast that the messenger trailed behind him.

Arrived at the Mayor's house, he found that the show of wisdom was to come before the feast. That was well. He might be sleepy after eating, and the three strangers did look most solemn and learned. Their heavy black

beards and the fur fringe of their long dark robes showed what distinguished men they were. He would have to be wide awake to appear as wise as they — wiser if possible.

"So this is the learned Hodja?" And the three priests looked him up and down. He wished he had taken time to put on his better clothes. He might at least have washed his face and straightened his turban.

"I will ask the first question," intoned one

of the priests as he stepped forward and fixed his piercing eyes on Nasr-ed-Din Hodja. "Where — is — the — center — of — the — earth?"

With the toe of his shabby shoe, the Hodja pointed to his donkey's left hind hoof.

"The center of the earth," said the Hodja, "is exactly under my donkey's left hind hoof."

"How can you be sure of that?" asked the priest, staring at the donkey's left hind hoof.

"Oh, I just know it," said the Hodja with a careless shrug of his shoulders. "Of course, if you doubt my answer, all you have to do is to measure. If your measuring shows the center of the earth is even an inch away from the place I say, I will know you are a greater scholar than I."

The visiting priest still stared stupidly at the donkey's left hind hoof. He shrugged his shoulders and motioned the next priest to take his turn.

"I have a question." The second priest had an I'll-catch-you-now expression in his steel-blue eyes. "How—many—stars—are—there — shining — at — night — in — the — sky?"

"There are as many stars in the heavens above," said the Hodja slowly, "as there are hairs on my donkey."

"How do you know that?" The stranger was staring at the shaggy coat of the donkey.

"Oh, it's just one of the things I know," shrugged the Hodja. "Of course, if you doubt my word, you may count the stars in the sky and count the hairs on my donkey. If there is one star too many or one hair too many, all Ak Shehir will know that you are a much wiser man than I."

The second priest stared stupidly at the donkey. He shrugged his shoulders and motioned to the third priest that it was his turn.

The third priest was the most important-looking of them all. His turban was the biggest. The fur fringe all the way up and down his robe was the heaviest. His beard was the longest. His expression was the smuggest.

"I have a very simple question for you, Nasr-ed-Din Hodja Effendi," said he in a voice that made the Hodja fear the question was not going to be so very simple. "How — many — hairs — are — there — in — my — beard?" He stroked his long black beard proudly.

"Oh, that is a simple question," agreed the Hodja. "There are as many hairs in your beard as there are hairs in my donkey's tail."

"How do you know that?" asked the priest, as he looked distastefully at the brushy end of the donkey's tail. He did not in the least fancy having his fine beard compared to that untidy tail.

"Oh, it's just another of those things that I happen to know," beamed the Hodja who was no longer awed by the solemn travelers. "Of course, you have the right to doubt my word."

"I do doubt your word!" snapped the priest, whose dignity was fast oozing away.

"That's quite all right," the Hodja said affably. "It will be simple enough to prove which of us is right and which of us is wrong. For every hair you pull out of my donkey's tail, I will pull one hair out of your chin. If the donkey's tail lasts even one hair after your beard is all plucked out, or if your beard lasts but a single hair after the donkey's tail is gone, you will be proved right and I will be proved wrong. If you are right, you can go from village to village, up and down the land, telling everyone you meet that you are far more learned than the humble Hodja of Ak Shehir."

Clapping both hands over his cherished beard, the priest drew back into the crowd.

And the Hodja wondered how soon the feast would begin.

THE WOODCUTTER'S HELPER

HIGH on a mountain trail, Nasr-ed-Din Hodja pulled his donkey to a sudden stop. The ring of an axe, the sound of a man's voice, and the tinkling of donkey bells told him there was companionship in this lonely spot. And the Hodja did like people who would talk and listen. He turned his donkey into a tiny footpath that led toward the sounds.

Soon he came upon a group of six donkeys grazing on some cleared land. On all sides were piles of wood cut into stove lengths. Near by was a muscular man swinging an axe. The woodcutter stepped quickly back as a pine tree swayed, moaned, and toppled to the ground. On a stump in the cool shade sat a neatly dressed man who clapped and applauded as the tree fell.

"Bravo, my strong woodcutter!" cheered
this second man who was not much more than
half the size of the woodcutter. "That was a
fine, big tree we cut. That will keep Siraj-ed-
Din Bey warm many a winter day. Haidi
bakalum! On to the next tree!"

Without looking at his comfortable companion, the woodcutter walked around an oak
tree to decide where it should fall, took a firm
grip on his axe handle, and started swinging
just above the tree's roots.

Each time the woodcutter's axe bit into the
tree, the little man on the stump would grunt.
The Hodja sat on his donkey, watching this
strange performance — the strong man swinging the axe without a sound passing his lips
while the sitting man kept up a steady flow of
grunts, groans, and cheers. It was too much
for the Hodja's curiosity.

"Why do you make all the noise while the
other man does all the work?" he asked the
little man.

"Oh, I am helping him," chirruped the man. "He has agreed to cut thirty donkey loads of wood for Siraj-ed-Din Bey. Think what a job that would be for one man. I took pity on him and went into partnership with him. He swings the axe while I grunt and cheer to keep up his courage."

The Hodja watched the woodcutter who was saying nothing, but making the chips fly. "I think," mused the Hodja, "it is the wood-

cutter's strong arms that give him courage."

The Hodja looked at the sun. It was growing late and he was not finding the two men very lively company. The Hodja gave the low throaty "Ughr-r-r-r," which started the donkey picking its careful way down the mountain trail toward home.

It was a fortnight later that the Hodja came upon the two men of the mountaintop again. He was loitering about the court, just in case the judge might need his advice about anything. It was amazing how often the Hodja's agile wit could pull the Judge's solemn wisdom out of a tangle. The two men of the mountaintop were disputing before the Judge. Their hands moved as fast as their tongues.

"I earned every ghurush of it myself," the big woodcutter was saying. "I did every stroke of the cutting of thirty donkey loads of wood for Siraj-ed-Din Bey. I loaded the wood onto the donkeys. I drove them to Siraj-ed-Din Bey's house, unloaded every stick of the wood alone, and went back to the mountain for more loads."

"He forgets!" the dapper little man of the stump interrupted. "He forgets how I cheered him at his work. I had a grunt for every swing of his axe, and a cheer for every falling tree. I earned a goodly portion of the money which Siraj-ed-Din Bey made the mistake of paying entirely to the woodcutter."

The Judge looked helpless. He had never met just such a case before. There was nothing in his law books about this kind of argument. He was relieved to see the familiar figure of Nasr-ed-Din Hodja elbowing its way through the crowd.

"I turn this case over to my able assistant, Nasr-ed-Din Hodja Effendi," said the Judge, sighing and leaning back, his troubles over. "Repeat your stories to the Hodja."

Both talking at once, the woodcutter and his self-appointed helper told their stories. The Hodja listened, nodding wisely, till both men

One by one the Hodja rang the coins on the tray

had talked themselves silent. Then the Hodja beckoned a court attendant.

"Bring me a money tray."

The tray was brought. The crowd pressed nearer to see what was going to happen.

"Give me the money, good woodcutter, the money Siraj-ed-Din Bey paid you for the thirty donkey loads of wood."

"But it is my money," pleaded the woodcutter. "I sweated and toiled for every ghurush of it while this man just sat in the shade and made strange sounds."

"The money, please," repeated the Hodja, holding out his hand for the bag. Reluctantly, the woodcutter passed over the money bag while the little man of the stump drew nearer, his eyes greedily aglitter.

One by one, the Hodja took the coins from the bag and rang them out on the money tray, talking to the man who was claiming a share.

"Do you hear that? Do you like the sound? Isn't that a cheery ring?"

The little man nodded, drawing so close that his nose almost touched the ringing coins. His thumb and forefinger were rubbing together as they itched for the feel of the money.

The last ghurush had left the bag and had made its cheerful ring on the money tray. The big woodcutter writhed to see his hard-earned wages in danger. The little helper smirked to see so much money so near.

"You heard it all?" the Hodja asked the little man.

He nodded hungrily.

"Every ghurush of it?" asked the Hodja.

The little man continued to nod.

"Then you have had your wages." The Hodja began to sweep the money back into the bag. "The sound of the money is proper pay for the sound of working."

The Hodja handed the full money bag to the smiling woodcutter, saying, "And the money is proper pay for the work."

FEET FOR ALL

THE boys of long-ago Turkey were as fond of jokes as boys of all times and all places have been. The boys of Ak Shehir had learned that a trick played on the cobbler might bring a piece of heavy leather flying at their heads. They knew that a trick played on the wagon driver might bring a lashing from his long whip. But a joke on Nasr-ed-Din Hodja was different. Nine times out of ten, to be sure, the joke would turn itself about and catch the boys instead of the Hodja, but it never hurt anyone. And there was always the hope that just this once the laugh would be on the Hodja. The boys never missed a chance to try.

One day four boys were wading in the brook

that flowed from the hills outside of Ak Shehir, when they heard the clip-clip of donkey's
hoofs.

"That sounds like Nasr-ed-Din Hodja's
donkey!" said Jemal, the baker's son.

Soon, along the path that followed the
brook, the watching boys saw a familiar gray
donkey with the good Hodja, half a doze, on
its back.

"The Hodja looks so sleepy, I'll bet we can
play a trick on him," said Nouri, the son of the
water seller.

"What trick?" asked Mahmoud, the candle-
maker's son.

"We must think fast!" said Ismail, the weav-
er's son.

The four boys stood in the middle of the
brook, with their heads close together. As
they schemed and plotted, Jemal happened to
look down into the water. He pointed and
whispered. The boys giggled. They shuffled
their feet about a bit and stood even closer

together, as they waited for the donkey and its sleepy rider.

The clip-clip of the donkey's hoofs came nearer and nearer. The boys stood as still as though their feet had taken root at the bottom of the brook.

"Shall we call to him?" whispered Mahmoud.

"He always speaks to us," answered Ismail. "If we let him speak first, he won't suspect anything."

The clip-clip of the donkey's hoofs stopped close to the boys.

"Good morning, youngsters!" said the Hodja. "What do you see in the water that makes you stand like trees growing in the brook?"

The boys nudged Jemal to speak.

"Oh, Hodja Effendi!" Jemal managed to make his voice sound like a distressed wail. "We are in the most terrible trouble! Aman, aman!"

"Trouble?" asked the Hodja, wide awake now. He jumped from his donkey, kicked off his loose shoes, and splashed into the brook beside the boys. "Trouble? Can I help?"

"We hope you can help," moaned Mahmoud. "If you cannot help us, no one can, and we must stand here in the brook till we are so old that our beards swish in the water."

"Oh, ne yapalim, what shall we do?" echoed Ismail.

The Hodja was peering into the water to find what terrible thing could have happened. All he could see was a tangle of eight sturdy legs and eight stubby feet. The boys nudged Jemal to go on with the story.

"Don't you see what has happened, Hodja Effendi?" groaned Jemal. "Our feet are completely mixed up. I think that foot and that foot are mine, but Ismail says one of those is his."

The boys all began to point at their feet and talk at the same time.

"I say that and that are mine, but Nouri claims one and Mahmoud claims the other."

"I know the biggest feet are mine, but Jemal says the biggest are his."

"I know I have a blister on my big toe, but Mahmoud is sure his is the foot with the blister."

The Hodja watched and clucked his tongue in a way that might have meant he was sorry for the boys. Or it might have meant something quite different. The boys were so busy talking and looking into the water that they did not watch the man they were trying to trick.

Nasr-ed-Din Hodja reached over to the brook's bank and picked up a heavy stick that lay there.

"I can help you find which feet are whose," said the Hodja as he plunged the long stick into the water right toward the tangle of feet. The stick stopped just short of where the feet had been, but it need not have stopped. No feet were there. They were all on the brook's bank, each pair safely attached to quite the right boy.

"So glad I could be of help to you, my young friends!"

With a rumbling chuckle, the Hodja shook the water from his feet, slipped into his shoes, and climbed onto his donkey's back. "Call me next time you lose your feet or get into some other sort of trouble."

The donkey carried the Hodja out of sight, but the four boys stood on the brook's bank. They were talking about that next time when they hoped the joke could be turned onto the Hodja.

THE HODJA AND THE HENS

FOR weeks the boys of Ak Shehir had been
itching to play a joke on their good friend,
Nasr-ed-Din Hodja. They had tried plenty
of times, but the Hodja had the most embar-
rassing way of turning jokes upside down so
that the laugh would be on the boys after all.
At last they had worked out a plan that could
not fail — at least it could not fail unless the
Hodja forgot to take a bath.

Finally, the day arrived, the day when the
Hodja would go to the Turkish bath to enjoy
a sociable time with his friends. Impatiently
he would wait for this day when he could go
for his weekly steaming and sudsing and scrub-
bing, and then for that delectable two hours or
so of relaxing on the high board sadir, all
wrapped up warm in his long burnous that

Fatima had bought in the towel market. This was the club of clubs, the time of times in which to visit and listen and luxuriate. Nasred-Din Hodja knew well how to do it all. So he went, his long black coat blowing out behind him as he trudged along.

Half a dozen boys joined the Hodja just before he reached the door of the public bath. They talked about this and that and the other — just not to seem too eager about their plan. Finally —

"I have an idea!" Nouri whacked Ismail on the back. "I have a wonderful idea! Let's pretend we are a flock of hens. The one who does not lay an egg in the bath will have to pay for baths for us all."

"Fine idea!" The boys were perhaps a little too quick to agree to such a strange plan.

"So you think you can lay eggs?" asked the Hodja.

"Of course!" agreed the boys, trying hard not to giggle. "Are you joining the game?"

"Surely. I'll be one of your flock." The Hodja could not guess what it was all about, but he did not intend to be left out of any fun — if it was to be fun. "If I don't prove myself as good a part of your poultry flock as any of you, I'll pay for all the baths."

As they undressed, the Hodja thought the boys were more slow and awkward than usual. He was ready first and followed the hammamji into the steam chamber.

There was nothing the Hodja enjoyed more than a peaceful time in the Turkish bath. He liked the warmth, the relaxation, the friendliness. All his worries, if he had any, seemed to flow away as the hammamji brought bowl after bowl of hot water for him. He loved to sing and hear his own voice magnified in the steam-laden air under the vaulted roof. His voice seemed as trilling and magnificent as the muezzin's own. Whenever he heard himself singing in the Turkish bath, he wondered why he had not studied to be a muezzin instead of a simple Hodja. Once he had been so impressed with his bath voice that he had climbed the twisting stairs of the minaret to try it from the high balcony. Out of the bath, his fine voice had been just a squeak and a croak. The people below had laughed, and he had called down to them that they should build him a Turkish bath on the minaret and then they would hear what a really fine voice he had. He forgot all about that today as he admired his voice floating through the bath.

The boys joined him, squatting beside him on the hot stones of the bath. Each boy held one hand closed lumpily, and did all his splashing with the other. They were very quiet, except for an occasional snort or giggle when nothing funny had happened as far as the Hodja could see. The Hodja was glad they were so still, because their quiet gave him more chance to sing and talk. The hammamji brought bowl after bowl of soothing, steaming water. Life was good — very good.

Suddenly one of the boys, squatting close to the Hodja, started a strange chant. "Cut-cut-ca-da-cut! Cut-cut-ca-da-cut!" The boy flapped his arms and jumped to his feet. He pointed to the hot stone where lay a smooth brown egg.

Before the Hodja had time to think, a second boy started the same strange chant. "Cut-cut-ca-da-cut! Cut-cut-ca-da-cut!" He too

flapped his arms, jumped to his feet and pointed to a smooth white egg that lay on the stone where he had been squatting.

One after another, the boys cackled, flapped their arms, and hopped up to show eggs. The Hodja remembered then how slow the boys had been to get ready for the bath so that he had been the first to leave the dressing room. The Hodja remembered too how they had each kept a hand closed lumpily as they squatted beside him. Their hands were wide open now as they hopped about in high glee.

"Your turn now, Hodja Effendi," they squealed. "Show us what a good member of our poultry flock you are, or you pay for all our baths." They were sure that, at last, they had outsmarted the Hodja.

The Hodja looked at the eggs, at the boys, at the hammamji. He looked about the steaming bath. Then he leaped onto a bench, stretched his neck as though he would try to touch the vaulted ceiling with his head, flapped his arms up and down at his sides and opened his mouth wide.

"Cock-a-doodle-doo! Cock-a-doodle-doo!" The Hodja's crowing echoed and re-echoed under the hot vaulted roof.

Then Nasr-ed-Din Hodja hopped calmly down from his perch, walked back to his seat, and motioned to the hammamji to go on with his work.

"In such a fine flock of hens," mused the Hodja, "you should have at least one good rooster."

And the boys paid for their own baths.

INSHA'ALLAH

NASR-ED-DIN HODJA stuck his bald head out of his bedroom window. He was studying the night sky, wondering what plans to make for the morrow. "What sort of weather do you suppose we'll be having tomorrow?" he asked.

"There'll be plenty to do whatever the weather." The busy Fatima was preparing their beds, taking the heavy mattresses from the cupboards, where they were kept during the day, and rolling them out on the floor. "If it rains, I shall weave, insha'allah. If the sun shines, I shall go to the river to wash the clothes, insha'allah."

"If it is pleasant tomorrow, I'm going to the fields to plow," announced the Hodja.

Fatima looked at him with warning in her

dark eyes. "Do not forget to say insha'allah, my good husband!"

Watching the clouds huddled over the horizon, Nasr-ed-Din Hodja ignored his wife's advice and went on. "If it rains tomorrow, I will go to the hills to chop wood."

"Speak carefully," Fatima warned again. "Never, never, never say what you will do without adding insha'allah!"

Nasr-ed-Din Hodja, less concerned than she about the customs that governed all good Turks, rolled onto his mattress, mumbling, "If it rains, I chop! If it shines, I plow!"

Fatima shook her head, worried. But, being far too wise to argue with a sleepy man, she blew out the poppy-oil lamp and felt her way to the mattress. Her sleep was troubled by dream after dream of the bad luck that might come to anyone bold enough to say what he would do without adding a protective "insha'allah." But Nasr-ed-Din Hodja slept as calmly and as loudly as his own donkey.

Morning showed that the clouds had won. There was a steady drip-drip of rain and a darkness of the sky that threatened more.

"This day I weave, insha'allah," said Fatima. She looked forward to a quiet day at her loom, creating inch after inch of cotton cloth with its gay stripes of blue and red and yellow. What a fine shirt it would make for Nasr-ed-Din Hodja.

"Today I chop," said Nasr-ed-Din Hodja. Not all of Fatima's beggings could induce him to so much as whisper "insha'allah."

So to her loom went Fatima. And, axe over shoulder, to the stable inside the strong street door went Nasr-ed-Din Hodja to mount his donkey and ride to the hills for wood. In the stable he found that his donkey had developed a lameness overnight. Nasr-ed-Din Hodja's first feeling was of relief. He would not have to work today! Surely no one could expect him to walk to the hills and carry the wood back on his own shoulders! Of course, he might command Fatima to come and carry the load; but that would stop the weaving of his shirt.

He started, humming happily, toward the house. The purr of Fatima's loom reminded him of something. He stopped. He turned slowly toward the street gate. How could he face Fatima if he failed to go to the hills to chop today? She would remind him that his donkey's lameness was a judgment on him for failing to say "insha'allah."

Through the gate and along the cobble-stoned streets of the town he shambled. Soon he was out on the rutted main road. He rolled up his long black robe to keep it out of the mud. He walked along slowly, head down, feet scuffling. Just one word of sympathy would have discouraged him completely and sent him scurrying home. But not one of his friends was there to say, "Poor Hodja Effendi, you should not be out on foot in such weather!" So on he plodded.

Good! There was a group of men at the

crossroads ahead.   Perhaps one of them would be kind enough to convince him that he might hurt himself if he insisted on going to the hills afoot.   Head up again, he walked hopefully toward the men, squinting in his effort to recognize them.   The nearer he went, the more he suspected that they were strangers — and soldiers at that.   From the way they were watching him, he began to wish he need not pass them; but it was too late to turn back.

"Here, you!"   One of the soldiers stepped directly in front of Nasr-ed-Din Hodja.   "Show us the way to Karabash!"

"Karabash?"   Nasr-ed-Din Hodja shook his head, trying his best to appear too stupid to know the way. "Karabash?"   He thought of the long turning road, going up and down hills, growing muddier with every drop of rain.   A stroll to the hills to chop wood began to look like a picnic compared to acting as guide for the soldiers.   "Karabash?"   He shook his head, trying to seem completely helpless.

"Oh, no! You don't fool us so easily!"
The soldiers fell on him with their fists. They
shook him. They pounded him. They
slapped him. "You lead us to Karabash!
March!"

Nasr-ed-Din Hodja cast a longing look at
the hills, where he could have spent the day in
the shelter of the woods, swinging his axe a
bit now and then. He cast a wistful glance
back at the cozy town of Ak Shehir, where

Fatima was sitting snugly at her humming loom.

Then, ducking his head so dejectedly that his turban seemed to rest on his shoulders, he took the path to Karabash. On and on he sloshed. The mud soon sucked away his shoes. It made such balls on his aching feet that he seemed to be wearing huge brown boots. The rain slapped him on the face. It beat upon his back. If he stopped for breath or to shake the mud from his feet, a soldier would be upon him, whacking him into motion again. He thought, when he was not too tired to think, of Fatima, the wise Fatima who had said, "I shall weave, insha'allah," and who was now sitting cozily before her singing loom. On and on he plodded. On and on and on —

It was nearly dusk when he at last stumbled through the gates of Karabash, the jostling soldiers close behind him. Not having a single friend within the walls of Karabash, and not having enough money to make even the faintest of jingling, he turned wearily back toward Ak Shehir. He pushed himself to make as much of the journey as possible while a flicker of daylight lasted. Twilight was short on so rainy a day.

Soon it was so dark that he must sometimes fall on his knees in the mud and feel with both hands to find the road. He was so tired that he would have used the soft mud for a mattress had not his sneezing warned him to press on toward home. He thought of Fatima in her dry warm house — the wise Fatima who had said, "I shall weave, insha'allah." On and on he plodded. On and on and on —

It was midnight when he at last stumbled over the welcome cobblestones of the streets of Ak Shehir. There were miniature torrents gushing between the stones, but they seemed dry and secure after the oozing mud through which he had been plowing. Wearily, he leaned against his own street gate and jangled the knocker to waken the sleeping Fatima.

"Who is there?" she called.

"Oh, Fatima," answered Nasr-ed-Din Hodja in a voice that was both small and cautious. "It — is — I — insha'allah!"

MONEY FROM THE SKY

OH, ALLAH! I need money! I need one thousand ghurush!" The wheedling voice of Nasr-ed-Din Hodja rose from behind his courtyard walls, built high of sun-dried brick of clay and straw. Whether or not the prayer rose to the ears of Allah, it was loud enough for the ears of the neighbors.

Siraj-ed-Din Bey, the wealthy merchant whose yard adjoined the Hodja's, looked from his upstairs window. He could see Nasr-ed-Din Hodja kneeling on a well-worn prayer rug, sitting erect, then bowing repeatedly till his forehead touched the ground, as he murmured his prayer again and again.

"Oh, Allah! I need money — much money. I need one thousand ghurush. Eight hundred ghurush would not be enough, nor nine hun-

dred, nor nine hundred and ninety-nine. I must have exactly one thousand ghurush. A smaller sum I could not possibly accept. Oh, Allah, send me one thousand ghurush — and may it come soon."

Siraj-ed-Din Bey, listening in his open window, smiled as he would have smiled at a child praying for a large piece of rahat lokum. He smiled at the Hodja's queer idea of prayer. Siraj-ed-Din Bey knew that if a man really wanted something, he had to mix work with his prayers.

The voice chanted on, "One thousand ghu-

rush, Allah!   Not one coin less than a thousand!"

"It is time to teach that simple old Hodja
not to pray without helping Allah to make his
prayers come true," thought Siraj-ed-Din Bey,
who was really fond of his kindly neighbor.
He laughed as a scheme grew in his mind.

Turning noiselessly from his high window,
Siraj-ed-Din Bey hurried to the room where
his money was hidden.   Carefully he counted
out nine hundred and ninety-nine ghurush.
He recounted it to be sure there was not a
single coin more or less.   He put the money
in a bag, tied it securely, and tiptoed back to
the open window.   His stockinged feet on his
thick rugs made not a sound.   Taking careful
aim, he tossed the money bag.   It barely
missed the Hodja's bowed head and landed
with a merry chinking on the cobblestones.
Then Siraj-ed-Din Bey hurried to his wife's
room, where he could watch unseen from behind her latticed window.

Without waiting to thank Allah, Nasr-ed-Din Hodja began counting the money. He counted it again and again. He tried to divide it into ten piles of one hundred ghurush each, but, no matter how many times he counted, one pile had but ninety-nine coins.

Siraj-ed-Din Bey and his wife, peering unseen through the latticed window, clapped their hands tightly over their mouths to hold back the laughter.

"I will let him count once more," whispered Siraj-ed-Din Bey to his wife. "Then I will explain the joke to him. He will laugh as hard as we."

But Siraj-ed-Din Bey had waited too long. Nasr-ed-Din Hodja did not count the coins again. Instead, he put them all snugly to rest in the money bag, tied the bag securely, and tucked it out of sight in his wide girdle. Then he knelt on the prayer rug.

"Oh, Allah!" prayed the Hodja. "You did not count the ghurush correctly. There were not quite one thousand. You owe me one more ghurush. Send me that whenever it is convenient. And thanks, many thanks, for the nine hundred and ninety-nine you did send me."

If it had not been for the lattice, Siraj-ed-Din Bey would have leaped through his window without bothering about stairs or gates. Passers-by gaped to see the wealthiest merchant of Ak Shehir rush from his door as though pursued by jackals and bang on Hodja's street gate. When the street door was pulled open for him, Siraj-ed-Din Bey shot through it toward the Hodja.

"Give me back my money bag!" shouted Siraj-ed-Din Bey, too excited to care who heard. He did not notice the open-mouthed crowd gathering at the Hodja's gate. "Give me back my nine hundred and ninety-nine ghurush!"

"Your money bag? Your nine hundred and ninety-nine ghurush?"

"Yes, mine! I tossed them over the wall

just for a joke. You said you would not accept less than a thousand ghurush. I was just trying to show you how silly such a prayer must sound to Allah."

"You tossed it? No, indeed! The money bag was a gift from Allah. It fell directly from heaven in answer to my prayer."

"I will take you and the money bag to court," said Siraj-ed-Din Bey, laying an angry hand on Nasr-ed-Din Hodja's shoulder. "We'll soon see whether it fell from heaven or from my window!"

"Yes, we'll have it decided in court." The Hodja always relished the court, with its chances for talk and excitement. "You will soon learn that this money fell from heaven."

"Well, hurry! Haidi bakalim!" Siraj-ed-Din Bey took a step toward the gate, but the Hodja hesitated.

"My coat! Fatima is mending it. I cannot go to court without it." The Hodja looked down at his shabby clothes.

"I will lend you a coat."

"But my donkey!   She has a lame foot.   I cannot ride her a long distance and, of course, we are in too much of a hurry to walk."

"I will lend you a horse."

"But a saddle and bridle!   My little donkey's would never fit your big horse."

"I will lend you a saddle and bridle.   Come into my yard and I will fit you out for the trip to court."

Nasr-ed-Din Hodja rolled up his prayer rug and put it away.   He waved good-bye toward his wife's latticed window.   He could not see her, but he knew her well enough to be sure she was not missing a word or a gesture.   Then he followed Siraj-ed-Din Bey.

In a short time the two men left the merchant's house on horseback.   The merchant had supplied Nasr-ed-Din Hodja with a spirited dappled gray, which he rode as though it were a donkey.   The Hodja bowed to left and to right as he went bouncing through the streets

The Hodja bowed to right and left

in his borrowed grandeur. He felt very high and mighty, but the men in the streets knew it would take more than an expensive coat, an embroidered saddle, a jingling bridle, and a fine horse to make a dashing horseman of the Hodja.

Arriving at the court, Siraj-ed-Din Bey lost no time in telling his story to the Judge. As he talked, he was disturbed at the strange way the Hodja was watching him, smiling sadly and shaking his head slowly.

"Well, Nasr-ed-Din Hodja," said the Judge, "have you anything to say?"

"Poor Siraj-ed-Din Bey," sighed the Hodja, his voice fairly dripping sympathy. "How sad! How very, very sad! He was such a good neighbor and so highly respected by all! To think that he should have lost his mind!"

"Lost his mind?" snapped the Judge. "What do you mean?"

"Oh, didn't you know?" The Hodja went close to the Judge and whispered in a voice that could be heard throughout the room, "He thinks everything belongs to him. You heard his story about my money bag. Just try him on something else, and he will be sure to say it is his. Ask him whose coat this is I have on my back."

"My coat, of course," exclaimed the merchant, not waiting for the Judge to ask. "The Hodja knows it is my coat."

The Hodja shook his head sadly. "Try something else, Judge. Ask him, for instance, whose saddle is on my dappled gray horse."

"My saddle, of course, and it's my bridle too," cried Siraj-ed-Din Bey. "The Hodja knows they are both mine."

"You see how pathetic it is," said the Hodja with a deep sigh of pity. "Poor man! He is so crazy that he might even claim my fine dappled gray horse."

"Of course I claim the horse," shouted the merchant. "I have owned that dappled gray since it was a colt."

The Hodja shrugged his shoulders. The Judge had evidence enough; let him decide.

"This is a strange case — a sad case," said the Judge thoughtfully. It was not easy to condemn the richest man in all Ak Shehir. "I believed Siraj-ed-Din Bey about tossing the money bag, though it was a rather wild story. Now I see differently. When he claims to own the Hodja's very coat and horse, saddle and bridle, he shows his mind is unbalanced. Siraj-ed-Din Bey, I suggest that you go home and take a good long rest. You have been working too hard, I am sure. Nasr-ed-Din Hodja, you may keep your money bag and all of your possessions that your unfortunate neighbor is trying to claim."

The two men rode in silence through the streets of Ak Shehir. Siraj-ed-Din Bey's shoulders sagged as though he had suddenly become an old man. Nasr-ed-Din Hodja bounced and gyrated with every step of the proud horse who was so unlike his donkey.

The merchant rode in at his own gate and turned to close it after himself. To his surprise, he was not alone. He was followed by the warmly grinning Hodja.

"Here is your money bag," said the Hodja, handing the heavy bag to the surprised merchant. "And your coat. And your horse with his saddle and bridle."

Siraj-ed-Din Bey, holding the money bag in one hand and the bridle of the dappled gray in the other, stared at the beaming Hodja, but could think of not a word to say.

"Wasn't it fun to fool that pompous old Judge?" chuckled the Hodja. "I'm going right back to court to tell him it was all a joke — that things are not always what the evidence makes them seem."

Siraj-ed-Din Bey revived quickly, to say, "Ride my horse back."

"Oh, no. My donkey's lameness is surely gone by now, and Fatima has probably mended my coat."

THE DONKEY EGG

FROM the folds of his loose jacket, Ali was bringing forth something large, smooth, round, and yellow. He held it proudly toward the Hodja and Fatima.

"A donkey egg," he announced. "All you need do is sit on this egg for three weeks. Then a baby donkey will hatch from it. He will grow and grow. In a few months you will have a second sturdy donkey to carry your loads and to take you both on journeys."

Nasr-ed-Din Hodja and Fatima were amazed at Ali's kindness. They had never thought of him before as a very good friend. In fact they had almost had a quarrel with him just the week before. And here he was planning how they could own a second donkey!

"We thank you up to the heavens and seven

times above the heavens!" they said as they kissed Ali's hand and pressed it to their foreheads. As Ali walked toward the gate, they called after him their promises to be his servants forever, in gratitude for this wonderful gift.

The next three weeks were long ones for Nasr-ed-Din Hodja and Fatima. While the Hodja sat on the donkey egg, his wife prepared the meals and cleaned the house and visited the neighbor women. While Fatima sat on the donkey egg, the Hodja went to the market place and chopped the wood and sat talking in the coffee house. Sitting on the donkey egg, the Hodja smoked his bubbling water pipe, or thought of wise advice to give to his neighbors, or nodded in a lazy doze. Sitting on the donkey egg, Fatima twirled her hand spindle until she had spun pounds and pounds of wool into scratchy yarn. The neighbors came in to talk to them. The men came when they knew the Hodja was sitting on the donkey egg. The women came when they knew Fatima was sitting on the donkey egg.

"Let us see the donkey egg," the neighbors would ask. "We have never seen one."

"Oh, no," Nasr-ed-Din Hodja or Fatima would reply. "We cannot take any chances of letting the donkey egg grow cold." And so it happened that from the time Ali brought the egg, no one saw it but the two who were so patiently and hopefully keeping it warm and dreaming of the little donkey that was to come from it.

A market day passed. A holy day passed. A bath day passed. The first week was gone. A second time the villagers brought their produce to the market place of Ak Shehir. A second time the men went to the mosque. A second time the people gathered at the public baths, the men in the morning, the women in the afternoon. The second week was gone. Another market day, another mosque day, another bath day marked the passing of the third

week. The Hodja and his wife knew that the time to look for their baby donkey had arrived at last.

They tapped cautiously on the donkey egg. It was much softer. Surely it would hatch soon. They patiently took turns sitting on the donkey egg through one more market day, one more mosque day, one more bath day. The egg was softer but no baby donkey had hatched from it. The softer the egg grew, the more peculiar was its odor.

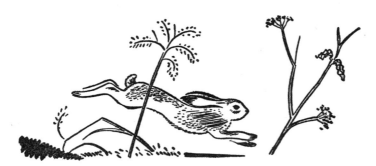

"This donkey egg is rotten," Nasr-ed-Din Hodja was finally forced to admit. "We can hope for no baby donkey."

Disappointed, he picked up the withered donkey egg to throw it away. As he walked slowly through the narrow cobblestoned street, he wondered why people looked so amused. The men smiled in such a queer way when they saw the donkey egg under his arm. The women tittered behind their veils and looked at each other. The children followed him, laughing and calling out something which finally settled into a rhythmic chant.

"Donkey eggs grow on pumpkin vines! Donkey eggs grow on pumpkin vines!" sang the children.

Too sad to notice what the children were saying, Nasr-ed-Din Hodja finally passed through the gate of the mud walls which surrounded the town. He stood at the top of a rough hillside and let his pumpkin, which he still thought was a donkey egg, roll down between the rocks and low bushes. As it rolled under a thorn-apple tree, it hit a stone and cracked open. A rabbit had been sleeping under the tree. Frightened by the bursting pumpkin, it went hopping down the hillside and disappeared. Seeing the long-eared rabbit leaping away, Nasr-ed-Din Hodja groaned.

"The baby donkey at last! The egg was just ready to hatch! Now our baby donkey is lost forever! Allah yardum etsin! May Allah help us!"

SOUP OF THE SOUP

WHAT a fine rabbit!" Nasr-ed-Din Hodja smiled as he took the plump rabbit that Hussein, the villager, held out to him.

"I caught it especially for you!" Hussein's smile was as broad as the Hodja's own.

"Fatima! Fatima!" called Nasr-ed-Din Hodja.

Pulling her scarf over her face, Fatima came bustling in from the kitchen.

"See what a feast Hussein has brought us!" The Hodja chuckled in anticipation of the good meal, as Fatima held out her hand for the limp rabbit. "I am asking him to stay and eat it with us. Cook it your very best!"

Left alone, the two men sat cross-legged on the floor and talked — at least, the Hodja

talked and the villager listened. The Hodja knew it would be nearly two hours before the meal was ready, but what better way to pass two hours than to have a quiet listener? Nasr-ed-Din Hodja's voice droned on contentedly. There were stories of his childhood, of his school days, of his exploits at the court of Tamerlane the Great, of the everyday news of his own city of Ak Shehir. There were his views of this, and that, and the other. Hussein, the perfect listener, knew just when to shrug his shoulders, to click his tongue, to wag his head, to rub his hands together. The pungent fragrance of roasting rabbit floated about them.

At last the door opened and in scuffled the veiled Fatima with a huge tray of rabbit and pilaf and a big plate of thin bread. She set the food between the two men and went scurrying back to the part of the house where a woman belonged when there were guests. Breaking off bits of bread, the men curved them into spoons and scooped up great mouthfuls of the steaming pilaf and rabbit.

"What a cook!" sighed Hussein. There was just the right touch of garlic, just the right sprinkling of pistachio nuts, just the right dryness of the rice.

"What a rabbit!" mumbled the Hodja, his mouth full to dripping.

They ate until their loose girdles were as tight as drumheads. They polished their plates with their bread to get the last succulent bit.

"There are still the bones left!" Nasr-ed-Din Hodja's voice was drowsy and contented. "Fatima's soups are as good as her pilafs."

Home to his village went Hussein, reporting to his neighbors how royally he had been treated at the home of Nasr-ed-Din Hodja.

The next morning, the Hodja was called to the door again. There stood two villagers — strangers. Remembering his treat of yesterday, the Hodja glanced quickly at their hands. Empty!

"What is your errand?" questioned the Hodja.

"We are the neighbors of the villager who brought you the rabbit yesterday." The men looked expectant. They seemed to be sniffing the air, which was already telling of the soup Fatima was preparing.

"Oh! A fine fellow is Hussein!" cried Nasred-Din Hodja. "Hosh geldiniz — your com-

ing gives joy. Any neighbors of his are welcome. Come in! Come in! Dinner will soon
be ready and you shall see what good soup
Fatima can make of the bones of the rabbit.
A great cook is my Fatima!"

Fatima, hearing the voices, padded softly
into the room and peered through her veil.
As she left the room, there were sounds behind her veil which might have meant, "What
fun to have guests again."   Or the sounds
might have meant something very different.

Soon Fatima brought in a tray with three
steaming bowls of soup, thick with rice and
vegetables and tiny shreds of rabbit meat.
She set the tray before the three men and
slipped out of the room. The Hodja talked
as he ate, but his stories did not flow with yesterday's enthusiasm.

The men thanked him for the meal and
went back to their village, to tell of the hos-
pitality of Nasr-ed-Din Hodja.

The next morning, the Hodja went warily

to answer a knock at the door. There stood
two other villagers — strangers again.

"And why am I honored with this call?"
Nasr-ed-Din Hodja had already glanced at
their hands and found them dangling empty
at their sides.

"We are the neighbors of the neighbors of
the villager who brought you the rabbit."
The two men grinned hopefully.

Nasr-ed-Din Hodja blinked, then said,
"Come in and share my humble meal."

The men walked in and squatted on the
floor while the Hodja went into the kitchen.
He poured a kettle of hot water over the
spoonful that remained of yesterday's soup.
He poured the liquid into bowls which he carried to the room where the men were waiting.

"Oh neighbors of the neighbors of the villager who brought me the delicious rabbit!"
Nasr-ed-Din Hodja's cordiality was loud.
"May you enjoy this soup of the soup of the
bones of the rabbit."

One neighbor of the neighbors of Hussein looked at his bowl of water in which two grains of rice swam beside a scrap of turnip. The other neighbor of the neighbors of Hussein looked at his bowl of water in which two grains of rice swam with a shred of onion and a chip of carrot. Nasr-ed-Din Hodja made a great noise of emptying his bowl before he smiled his guests to the door.

And the next day Fatima and Nasr-ed-Din Hodja sat down to a quiet meal together once more.

ACKNOWLEDGMENTS

We thank the missionaries of Merzifoun, Turkey, for introducing us to the Nasr-ed-Din Hodja cycle of Turkish folklore. Dr. and Mrs. George E. White, Rev. and Mrs. Dana K. Getchell, Dr. and Mrs. Jesse K. Marden, the Rev. and Mrs. Ernest Pye, Mr. and Mrs. Theodore Riggs, Bertha Morley, Fanny Noyes, Mary Ward, Charlotte Willard, and Emma Zbinden loved Turkish folkways and Turkish folklore. They passed the love of them on to some of us who went to Merzifoun in 1919 to do relief work.

We might have forgotten the Hodja had he not followed us to America when some of our Merzifoun orphans grew to college age and made their headquarters with us while studying here. Haig Baronian, Charalambos Stephanides, Demetrius Photiades, and Charalambos Panayotides entertained our four children with the tales about Nasr-ed-Din Hodja. Enjoying these stories with our children, we became avid Hodja fans and begged for Hodja stories whenever we had visitors from the Near East. Among the students, missionaries, and welfare workers who have added to our stock of Hodja stories are Jeanette Odell, Merrill Isely, Paul Nilsen, Nevzat Jemal, Herman Kreider, and Ralph Allee.

We have compared these stories as told us with those in the German collection by Ali Nouri and in the translation of the Hodja stories into English by Henry D. Barnham.

Special gratitude goes to the Rev. and Mrs. Ernest Pye for reading the manuscript. From their background of first-hand knowledge of the Near East, they were able to correct inaccuracies and add bits of local color.

Apologies go to the many people who could have written the Hodja stories better than I. My only excuse is that I spent nearly twenty years saying, "Someone ought to write the Nasr-ed-Din Hodja stories for American boys and girls," before I decided that I would have to do it myself.

ALICE GEER KELSEY

Ithaca, New York
July, 1943

GLOSSARY

The author has used a phonetic spelling nearest approximating the Turkish sounds.

Ahmet: Most laudable; a name often given Turkish boys.

Ak Shehir: White City; a city in Asia Minor.

Allah: Arabic name for the Deity.

Allah eekbar: God is great. The first words of the Moslem call to prayer.

Allah yardum etsin: May heaven help us!

aman aman: Woe is me!

baklava: Turkish sweet pastry.

Bey: Title for civil functionaries and any person of distinction.

burnous: An Arabian cloak, robe.

dervish: Moslem religious enthusiasts.

dolmas: Meat and rice cooked in tomatoes, green peppers, grape or cabbage leaves.

Effendi: Title applied to persons of scholastic or official rank.   Also a term of courtesy among equals.

Fatima: A woman's name.

ghurush: Turkish money.   In paper currency equal to less than one cent American money.   In gold currency it is equal to $4\frac{4}{10}$ cents.

haidi bakalum: Let's get going!   Come!

hammamji: The director of a public bath.

Hassan: A name often given to boys.

hosh geldiniz: Your coming gives joy; welcome.

Hodja: Teacher, master or elder.

insha'allah: If God is willing; I hope so.

Ismail: Ishmael, a boy's name.

Jemal: A boy's name.

khayr olsoun: How do you do?

Koran: Mohammedan holy book.

lira: One hundred ghurush.

Mahmoud: A boy's name, meaning "praise-worthy."

mash Allah: An expression used after praise or good luck to ward away the evil eye.

Mehmet Ali: A boy's name.

muezzin: Priest who gives call to prayer from minaret.

mongal: Small, open-topped stove.

Nasr-ed-Din: Boy's name meaning "favored of religion."

Nemaz: Divine worship in Islam, including recitals of praise with prostrations of the body.

ne yapalim: What shall we do?

Nouri: A name often given to boys.

pilaf: Rice or wheat cooked in meat or vegetable broth.

rahat lokum: Turkish delight, a candy similar to gum drops.

sadir: Couch.

selamun aleykum: Peace be with you!

Tamerlane: Mongol conqueror.

vai, vai: Woe is me!

ve aleykum: "And unto you be peace," the reply by a Moslem to the greeting of another in the faith.

ONCE THE HODJA

By

ALICE GEER KELSEY

Illustrated by

FRANK DOBIAS

WITH the appearance of *Once the Hodja* a new folk character is introduced to American children. He comes from Turkey where Turks of all ages love to hear and tell stories of him. A simple kindly country fellow, with a talent for getting into trouble, he has even greater talent for getting out. Bait for small boys and grown men-alike, the Hodja almost always, but not quite always, turns the table on those who would make a scapegoat of him. Seldom has a more genuinely humorous and appealing folk character been presented.

Most countries have some character on which to hang funny stories and Turkey has Nasr-ed-Din Hodja. The historical Hodja lived about five centuries ago, but the legendary hero is very much alive today. Out of a living knowledge of Turkey and a warm affection and sympathy for the Hodja himself have come this delightful collection of folktales. For this volume Alice Geer Kelsey has selected from the hundreds of stories about the Hodja those that have the most spontaneity and humor — that have stood the test of telling and retelling and she has woven them into a background that makes the reader at home in mosque, public bath, market place, vineyard or the Hodja's home.

Like the author, Frank Dobias has lived in Turkey. His illustrations have caught the lively, contagious, laughing spirit of the Hodja stories.

No. 25

$3.59